Dedication

To all of those that supported me and believed in me, I can't express my appreciation enough, thank you from the bottom of my heart!

To those that doubted me; including myself:

This should show you!

Glass Screams

L. R. Claude

ISBN: 0-6157-8586-7
ISBN-13: 9780615785868

Contents

Glass Screams

February 25th 2012 was when my life was changed forever, Cliche I know but it's true. My name is Lorna Daniels and I was in a major car accident and that was just the beginning. I don't know how the rest of my life may turn out but keeping this journal is a recommendation of my therapist to help me with my nightmares while I am trying to recover. I am fourteen and spent March trapped in the upper crust of hell and when April turned over, a new nightmare arose from which I may never be able to wake up.

I am fourteen and in my eighth grade year of middle school, I was out at the end of February with my sister Sara, and her best friend Katie, in Kalamazoo for a "Lady A" concert. The concert was great, Rucker was fantastic and played a list of great songs, and the headliners were so charged with energy. The three of us just danced during the upbeat songs and cried during the slow romantic songs, in hopes of one day dancing to the very same songs, in our futures with the loves of our lives.

The three of us girls gorged on soft pretzels and stale concert nachos, binged on Diet Pepsi and over indulged on great country music. I wore my favorite jean skirt with my white leggings underneath, a purple plaid shirt and a matching hair tie, I was so cute. My older sister Sara wore her new black leather boots with dark jeans and a nice collared blouse. Katie, Sara's best friend, was wearing a Pink hoodie with light blue jeans, we were all looking just as cute as could be. The concert was loaded with cute country boys and so many people wearing cowboy hats and boots.

That was my first concert and a night I'll never forget. We left for the concert around eleven that Friday. The concert was to be a great time with Katie and Sara as we laughed, wondered what the concert would be like that night and joked. We talked about teachers and how stupid boys have become. One of the boys in my history class had just received detention, on a Friday, for tossing pencils into the fake ceiling stuff in class, our teacher was only out of the room for four or five minutes and he managed to flip six pencils up there. Scott was only caught because one of the pencils fell and hit his desk as she restarted her lecture.

We spent the two hour drive on our to the concert texting the 'rents to ensure we were maintaining proper speeds and safety. Sara had gotten her license in November and this was her second time driving out of the city. Mom and dad were leery about us going so far from home but the roads weren't icy and snow wasn't in the forecast. Sara's Ford Focus was an awesome Christmas present or at least the other half haha. Mom and dad were very cool about her getting a car, they met her half way on the financing it part but a car meant freedom no matter what.

We stopped and ate not long after 5pm in Battle Creek, which was about half way between Jackson and K-Zoo and for the relief of the 'rents that Sara not make the hour plus drive in one stretch. We stopped off at Applebee's and ate lightly. Sara had the rib tips, Katie the chicken and I had an awesome chicken wrap, and it was so yummy. We headed back onto I-69 just before six and back to laughing and giggling as we were before the dinner stop. We could tell we were nearing the right exit for the State venue, traffic was unbearable but we had plenty to keep us busy.

I was texting my friend Bobbi, whom was bummed she couldn't go with us but she understood. The tickets were a gift to Katie to take Sara and their other friend Kelly but Kelly couldn't go due to last minute flu issues, CONCERT for me!!! Sara offered to drive since Katie only had her license a week and also didn't have a car yet. I know I was a last minute add-on to the road trip but Sara and I got along great and both she and Katie have been a huge help getting through middle school. School was OK and all the girls started getting real catty and the boys seemed to slump backwards, beyond immaturity and into that realm just above dogs that tried to hump your leg every time you stood still.

Suddenly farts became funnier than in fifth grade, boobs seemed to be the biggest topic, and most of the boys seemed to be wearing clothes that were eight sizes too big. These scruffy pants-sagging boys suddenly couldn't even see many girls in our grade, they followed around the girls that started to develop breasts and lather on the make-up with paint rollers. I had just started to change physically and all I know is that things itch and all you can do is notice which friends develop faster and try not to be crazy self-conscious about everything.

Things were all out of whack, I know I grew six inches over the last year or so, half of my school pants became capris this year already and my feet grew the most, they don't seem to work as well as they're supposed to and I feel like such a klutz. Katie was super sweet, she had an older brother named Ryann and he was one of the nerdy quiet guys that dressed grungy so she didn't have anyone to help lead her through the physical morphing mess and sorta started to look out for me.

Katie seemed to love having a younger sister and even when Sara was at the end of her patience with me, Katie would step up and quell the heat, she was so awesome. I enjoy having them both as my older sisters. Katie was into Varsity Blues and could sing so well, she loved Underwood and Swift and she was always smiling her big toothy grin. Sara was an awesome cross country runner, she had reached her thousand mile mark midpoint in her junior year and we were all so proud of her.

I learned a lot from hanging out with them, Bobbi also was included into our raga muffin style family. The four of us spent a lot of time together, Katie usually came and hung out with us after school while her father worked and Sara was out running. Bobbi and I ran track in the spring but to be honest I wasn't a fan of running, but I liked to spend the time with Bobbi anyways. We also supported Katie and her beautiful talent with singing and performances within the Varsity Blues experience. I loved how close we were and last names didn't matter, we were all sisters.

We got into the concert; the theater place was so crowded. I had never been to a concert before so I was kinda nervous, we were sardined into corrals like cows. I must have had my butt grabbed five or six times and each time I turned around to see who it was, some old pervy guy was always there, it was so gross. We got to our seats and we were so close, it was amazing and I was so excited for the show to start. The first performer played and was a substitute for the scheduled band but he was funny and goofy between songs, he spoke to the fans in the crowd and I recognized a few of his songs from the radio.

The second performer "Rucker" played and he really got the place jumping, he not only played his great songs but also threw in songs like "Mountain music" by Alabama and "Purple Rain" by Prince, it was such a great time. The headliners started and that's when things really went berserk. All the girls hooted and hollered and all the fellas were waving hats and lighters. During the show lots of guys would dance in their small areas with their gals and it was really romantic to see all sorts of people from all over scooting and swaying their bodies in rhythm. Katie sang along and some of the seat neighbors that could hear her over the bass and level of the music would turn to see this beautiful sixteen year old girl sing just as well as the big name musicians up on stage.

Between songs we would duck out to the main hall full of vendors and grab snacks as well as rotate bathroom breaks. First break, Katie and I snuck into the restroom while Sara was on pretzel round up. Second time Sara and I went while Katie scored us nachos. It was such a great time. The concert went so fast and seemed to be absolutely filled with energy. The show was great and before the mid show intermission we each agreed on which tee shirt we would get. The shirts were expensive but we each agreed to buy a different one and then swap and share so none of us would have to go without one that we each wanted.

The night seemed to be enthralled with beauty, the hats, the music, the heart and soul lifting lyrics that seemed to be applicable to so many instances in our young lives already. They say money can't buy you happiness but buying music and going to concerts sure seems as close as possible. The bathroom lines were a terror, just absolute insanity. The boys' bathroom line was just as long but they had the ability to be quick with the standing to pee and what not. The last bathroom break was over and we agreed to catch the last few songs afterwards so we wouldn't have to get back in the car with bladders full of Pepsi and wait for what seemed like a month to exit the parking lot.

The ending of the concert was so beautiful; they pulled a little girl onstage with them and serenaded this little girl with their newest big hit. The little girl was so overwhelmed that she cried and seeing that little girl have the time of her life and crying over it caused all of us to cry, it was so sweet. I know I'll never forget that night and I hope that little girl remembers it forever also.

We gathered our jackets and put our new shirts on over the tops we were wearing and started on the slow paced, bumping and grinding that was the journey to our exit. I was following Katie real quick while Sara had her hand and was leading us out of that mess. I caught a few smiles from some of the cute cowboys; one boy had some dimples that made me feel flush in my face almost instantly. It was boob to elbow for what seemed like an hour, toes stepped on and butts grabbed, when we finally got out, Sara won the "who got groped the most" game haha.

It took us a few minutes to make our way back to the car, it was freezing outside. We had gotten all hot and sweaty during the concert with the dancing and jumping and now that we hit that cold February Michigan air, it was brisk. We ran the last twenty feet to Sara's little blue Focus, we called it Shelly. We sat in Shelly and listened to concert coverage by the local radio station and listened to people talk about the passion and energy put out tonight onstage and the collective energy that was being put out from the crowd. What an awesome night.

We followed what seemed to be the fastest moving line to snake our way back to I-69 to head east back to Jackson. The line just to exit the parking lot, every time we seemed to slide over to a faster moving line, came to an abrupt stop, all we could do was laugh about that dilemma. We followed in line behind a big stinky truck, the parking lot seemed to be a collection of trucks, jacked up rigs with lights and bars in the back, cowboy hats with boys underneath them hooting and hollering every chance they got.

We were propositioned a few times to flash some of these boys. My sister is a tall thin brunette and a very pretty girl. Katie is also tall and thin with short blonde hair so between the two of them in front I was subjected to a lot of "cat calls" and some vulgarity between vehicles. We laughed them off and laughed even harder at some of the boys in the beds of the trucks mooning other cars and watching some of the flag flying goofy guys dancing and jiggling in the beds of some of these trucks. I don't understand how some of these steamy shirtless guys were acting so foolish in the beds of these trucks driving past sheriffs and state troopers escorting vehicles out towards the streets to safely decongest the lot.

We followed the GPS on Sara's phone to get to the interstate and I texted mom that we were off and moving, she replied with "east bound and down?" mom was silly like that. Sara and Katie started talking about some of the cute boys in tight plaid shirts they had noticed at the concert. Katie always mentioned wanting to someday marry a country boy. We had a great time and that was the point of that night. Kelly was really bummed out that she had to forgo the night with Katie and Sara, I felt bad enough for her loss that I bought her a shirt also.

I texted Bobbi on and off that night, what songs they played, seeing some goofy people and several no sleeved bearded good ole boys, some of the girls wearing way too little and the masses and masses of cowboy hats. Bobbi said I should have encouraged Katie to flirt with some of the younger cuties but we were all too shy, besides, what good would it have done? We lived too far from this point and people came from all over the state and then some. We saw license plates from Indiana, Illinois, and Ohio.

It took a good three or four exits for us to be able to thin the traffic out enough to be on our way comfortably. We were surrounded by many of the same trucks on the highway that were in the parking lot. Many of the same trucks that had rowdy boys being silly had calmed down a lot by that point during the drive. We talked about some of the boys in one Ford truck that were dangling in the back mooning people were now laying against the window sleeping as the slow and quiet set in. During our drive we too settled down from a wild and crazy night.

We enjoyed that we were in the thralls of our youth. We poked fun at each other and talked more about middle school. Katie and Sara spoke about how they ruled eighth grade and at the top of their social pyramids only to get knocked back down and have to re-climb that mountain come freshmen year. I was intrigued to hear their tales and tell it how it was so I knew what I was in for. Katie had some older class girl pick on her for her short hair most of her freshmen year. Katie was a strong girl having been raised by her father with her brother Ryann. Ryann had some low life friends and her father wrenched on cars for a living so she had a thick skin.

Ryann was quiet and dressed in grungy clothes but that was his style, Katie dressed very nice and always looked super cute. Eighth grade wasn't the most fun but Katie and Sara reassured me that that's how eighth grade was, no more and no less. I had plenty of support from them, during track season I jogged with Sara during her short runs, two miles or less and I could keep up but then my legs and lungs burned and I'd slow up and head back home and she would kick up her heels and take off for another five or six miles. I really enjoyed history and social studies and planned to keep those subjects in my educational future.

We were on our way home and Katie was just going to stay the night with us. Katie lives just down the block but she stayed over quite a bit because she lived with two guys, I couldn't blame her a single bit. The radio turned into static as we got farther and further from Kalamazoo so we just turned the volume down and kept chatting and giggling away into the night.

chapter 2

BAMMMMM!!! WE HAD come close to Battle Creek and decided to pass right on through. We were making good time and hadn't passed the exit but a few minutes when the truck on our right side had suddenly veered into us. Screeching, crashing, crunching, shattering, soul shaking sounds completely consumed us. All the windows seemed to explode at the same time; glass went flying and sprayed us in our faces. I remember seeing a bright headlight over my right shoulder on the passenger side.

The truck slammed into Katie's door and the entire car felt like it was lifted a thousand feet into the air and slammed back down. There was another slam as we hit the inner cement guard wall on the highway and then "BOOM BOOM BOOM" as the air bags went off throwing more glass at us from all angles. The loud SCHSSSS of the breaking glass continued as other windows shattered, spraying shards onto us. I couldn't see anything as I felt like I was being sprayed with water but I could hear Sara screaming. This little car suddenly felt open, airy and smoke burned by lungs. My head was whipped around and my body slammed against the seat belt over and over, my legs began to burn and my neck felt like it had been ripped off. I couldn't feel my body, I could hear Katie crying. I could hear tires still screeching then another slamming blow to the car.

BOOM we got hit again. All this seemed to last for hours. It might have been over in mere seconds but the screaming glass, crying tires, metal crunching and growling all around us seemed to chew on us. My body hurt all over. I couldn't see, I felt wet and cold suddenly biting at my face. My arms wouldn't move. I couldn't unbuckle my seat belt, I couldn't lift my feet. My head hurt and my long hair was covering my face. I could tell that I was leaning but mostly upright. If it wasn't for Sara's screaming gurgling cries I wouldn't have been able to tell she was there. Katie had a muffled cough in her crying. Katie was coughing and sounded like she was throwing up. My eyes wouldn't open, they burned and my body felt like it was on fire.

Sara was trying to scream for help but crying too hard to form understandable words. I was crying and I hurt too. My body wouldn't move, I was trapped and pinned and I was trying to scream but all I could hear was that twisting metal noise shrouding my thoughts. All I could see in my mind was that flash of light and my body kept feeling like it was being jolted over and over again. Sara got quiet. I couldn't stop sobbing, my body jerked and everything burned. I couldn't reach my phone.

I felt my eyes suddenly open and my head jilt backwards into the headrest of the seat. I still couldn't see anything and my face felt soaked and my hair matted to me. My body still wouldn't move, I tried to move my hands but couldn't feel them. I began to panic and cry out for my mom. Why wasn't my mom there? I needed her to make everything alright. I was so scared and worried and I couldn't move.

I couldn't seem to scream loud enough, why wasn't anyone listening? Why wasn't anyone helping? My body was shaking but I wasn't cold. I couldn't move. Was I dead? What was happening? Where were we? Why couldn't I hear Katie or Sara? Where were they? What was going on? Am I paralyzed? What happened? That bright flash kept flashing in my mind and my body kept jolting. Where was my mom? I wanted my mommy. I'm crying and no one can hear me.

That song "Last Kiss" by J. Frank Wilson and the Cavalier's is playing in my head. I heard that song last fall in the garage one night when I was helping my dad pull wires through a wall thingy with him on his project car. That song was so sad and it made me well up. I tried not to cry but dad caught me. Dad said oldies had feelings in them that people seemed to lack nowadays. My hands were small enough to feed wires through a small hole in the car and it was tedious to do but it was time I got to spend with dad, just us.

The loud bang and crunching metal kept ringing in my ears. My body wasn't moving. I could feel my lungs burning with smoke and hot air. Was I burning to death? Was the car on fire? I can't feel anything, not the seat, not the seatbelt, not my arms or legs; I can't feel my hands or feet moving. I can't hear Sara or Katie, are they OK?

I jolted again and could feel my head move and once again hit the headrest. My body shook and my heart was pounding, I thought it was going to explode like I had just run a hundred mile marathon; downhill. I could feel the seatbelt squeezing me. I could feel tears running down my face; I can't be dead if I'm crying right? I can feel my shirt soaked and the glass stinging my body. My whole body felt like the pins and needles feeling you get when your foot falls asleep. I could taste the metallic bloody taste in my mouth. I could feel glass in my mouth. Every breath burned and I swear my chest was going to explode.

My lungs wouldn't inflate to let me scream. I tried yelling out but I couldn't hear anything. My whole right side felt hot. My face felt warm and wet. What happened? Where is everyone? Aren't people supposed to be helping? I can't hear sirens or people talking or screaming or crying. Why weren't Sara or Katie talking or crying? Where were they?

My body jolted again. I felt wet running down my face. I couldn't feel my body or anything move, just my chest tightening with each breath. I tried to make a fist but couldn't feel any of my muscles move, was my arm still there? Oh god did I lose my arm? I can't feel my legs, am I paralyzed? Did something happen to my body? Am I dying? Where is my mommy? I'm so scared.

I smell smoke and chemicals. It smells like hot plastic, like burned batteries. Why can't I open my eyes? I can feel my heart pounding again. My throat hurts from inhaling this chemical smoke. My neck hurts and it feels like I got kicked in it. Will I be ok? Will I make it back to school? Will I see my parents again? Will they know how much I love them? Will I ever get to go for a run with Sara again? What is happening? What happened to Sara or Katie?

I kept jolting forward and my body shook like one of those paint shaker things I saw at Lowes when I went with my dad when we repainted my room last summer. It was dark but I could feel warmth on my face, why couldn't I see anything? Am I blind? What is going to happen with me? Where is my phone? Why won't my hands work? My face feels flush and hot.

MMMM, I heard someone moan, I think it was Sara. My heart pounding is giving me an awful headache. I can't stop crying. My body keeps jolting and each time the pins and needles keep hurting all over. A sudden pain from my lower back spiked and climbed all the way up my spine and I tried to scream again. I keep trying to yell for help but I can't catch a breath. My lungs burn so badly. The glass screams keep echoing in my head. The flash of light followed by the growl of metal keeps filling my ears. I can't hear anyone talking or shouting. I can't hear any sirens? Does anyone know we are here?

I keep trying to yell for Sara, I don't know if she's okay, I don't know if I'm ok. Where are we? How are my parents going to find us? Where is my mommy? I remember falling off my bike and hitting a fence post and my mom was right there to hold me and reassure me that I was ok when I was younger, I want her here. I want my dad's strong arms to pick me up like he used to when I was a little girl. Why can't I scream? My face feels wet, puffy and my body hurts.

I jolted again and the pins and needles hurt and my body is shaking so bad, I can't feel myself moving. My heart is thumping like a bass drum. I can't hear the radio, I can't feel my hands. I can't breathe. My neck hurts and my head hurts and my body isn't working, it's like it's not even there anymore. If I could just see that I'm in one piece and that Sara and Katie are ok. God why can't I see or hear them?

Oh god I was in a car accident, pictures of wrecked cars, entangled masses of metal, fabric and tires are filling my head. That flash of light and tearing metal and concussive breaking glass are flashing in my head like a strobe light at an awful haunted house. I want to see my parents, I want to go running in the summer with Sara, I want my body to work and get me out of this hell. Was I not a good enough daughter, friend, sister? What would have happened if Kelly was here instead of me? Oh god am I wishing someone one else was in this seat instead of me? Am I a horrible person because I wish this wasn't me?

I haven't even kissed a boy. What if I die without knowing the kind of love that inspires some of the great songs I heard tonight? Did I deserve this? Was I going to live? What if I lose my leg, or my arms? Will I be able to hug my mom or dad ever again? My lungs hurt. Everything seems muffled. I feel numb but everything hurts. The pressure on my chest needs to stop. My heart is still pounding and I can feel each heavy beat in my head. How long have we been here? How long will we be stuck in this car? Am I going to die tonight?

What if I won't get to help hold work lights for my dad as he works on his beloved sixty-five mustang? What if I won't get to have any more all girls shopping sprees with my mom and Sara? I loved doing so many things, what if this is it? Am I going to die? Am I going to become one of those girls, people that you hear about dying young and then only being remembered by their parents? Then one day just being "that girl who died"?

My body jolted again, this time violently lurching forward. I felt the seatbelt against my chest and lap. I felt some of my body, my stomach is tight and hurts, is the seatbelt crushing me? My lungs hurt and I can't breathe, am I going to suffocate? "*Mommy?*" I'm trying to call out, for mom or for Sara. I can't hear myself shouting, I can't hear anything except that crushing metal sound ringing in my ears and the sharp crackling of the glass.

The exploding glass screams in my brain, there is no silence around me. Are we still crashing?

Am I dead? Am I going to spend forever without the feeling of my body, entombed in the symphony of nightmarish destructive agony that is replaying in my mind? My face feels heavy, wet and warm. Images of car accidents flash in my mind, is my car now just another picture online, mangled and the final point that a few young girls lost their lives in? A story that other parents will read and point out to their kids like mom and dad did to Sara and me? Will they have an assembly at school like they have in the past? One where kids will joke and snark and make comments about how they'll be too smart to text and drive or just say "it won't happen to me" and they'll dismiss the entire thing?

Will Bobbi find a new best friend? Another girl that will braid her hair, to share music or makeup tips with? Will my pink room be converted to a gym for my dad or a sewing room for my mom or end up a shrine to the memory of a lost daughter? Will my parents get through burying their daughters together or will the overwhelming emotions take its toll on their great marriage and send them both spiraling apart? What if I can't ever walk again? What if I'm paralyzed and can't ever dance or jump again? Why can't I feel anything but pins and needles?

The flash of lights strobe through my mind again and the wretched metal sound causes me to jerk again. I still can't lift my eyelids, I can feel my eyebrows trying but they feel like they weigh a ton. My eyelids are stuck together and won't open. Where is my mommy? Daddy? Somebody please help us. Sara, are you ok? Katie, are you there? Why won't anybody answer? Is anybody there? Can anyone hear me? Is Sara dead?

Why aren't any people helping? I'm so scared, I don't want to die. Am I an amputee? Is this what it feels like to die? Am I bleeding to death? I'm sure we were in a car accident, what happened? My mind is screaming and racing with each thumping pounding heartbeat. LUB DUB LUB DUB, each pounding pulse echoes in my ears mixed with the muffled crackle and thunderous booms of explosions. Why aren't there any sirens or people yelling to figure out if we're ok? Where's the help? Where's my mom?

It seemed like an eternity, trapped in that position. Forever was upon me as I was stuck, my head felt heavy, my eyes wouldn't open. My lungs burned with the weight of my chest increasing as each breath made me work harder and harder to grasp. Where the hell is everyone? Why aren't people doing anything? I want to scream for help, I want to scream to make people do something, anything.

I don't understand why this is taking forever. In the movies emergency people scurry around and saved people in the flashing lights and yelping wail of sirens. It was silent. Maybe this is really the end for me. Maybe this is the end of me and my story. Will I die without leaving any amazing stories to be told, just a generic young girl with no adventures to speak of? I've been on vacations with my family, the four of us spent a few days biking around Mackinac Island and a few winters living the winter wonderland that is Frankenmuth. I loved the fall cherry festival in Traverse City, yes we were some of the thousands of touristy families that added to the crowds of spectators but it was our family and we made each trip special in our own ways.

Michigan offered so many amazing things to experience as a family and we partook in being Michiganders with pride. The old architecture of Detroit and the stories of Dad talking about the once prosperous hustle and bustle of Detroit and going with his dad to watch the Tigers play. We visited what he called the new stadium a few times a summer, Sara and I didn't have much interest in playing ball but watching the Tigers play in such a grand arena and the bright hues of the grass seemed so magnificent.

One time dad picked me up from school, just he and I, he asked if I wanted hot dogs for lunch, I'm not the biggest fan of hot-dogs but he said dogs are always better field side, and we went and watched a midday game one Thursday in early June last year. I loved spending time outside with dad. Dad was so knowledgeable and he had so much to teach me, even when I wasn't interested in some things, like his rebuilding of his mustang. I'll never get to ride in the finished car.

I could taste blood and metal and feel shards of glass cutting my gums. The chemical smell and taste seemed overpowering at times and I couldn't focus on anything else. My body seemed to shiver uncontrollably, like being super cold and having one of those chills you can't shake off. Will I look beautiful in my casket? What will I be dressed in? Will it be in something satin like that song? My chest and stomach muscles seemed to spasm, like my legs did after hard runs with Sara.

Is Katie ok? Is Sara ok? Everything is dark black, my face feels heavy and wet, my chest burns and stings. Can you hurt if you're dead? What if it's like those situations you read about that your brain keeps working after you've died? Is my brain going at a million miles an hour but my body has died or maybe I'm dying but I don't realize it? If I'm dead how will I know? Will I fade into sleep or just cease to live? Will it all just fade to black?

My body jerked again. I could feel my shoulder move a little that time and my chest muscles flex like it did when I had to do push-ups during that presidential fitness thing at school. I couldn't do more than five push-ups. Amber W. could do sixteen push-ups, why couldn't I do very many? Sixteen is a lot. Why am I thinking of so many things?

Oh god, is this my life flashing before my eyes? Why haven't I thought about my grandparents? Oh my grandparents, Nan, Papp and Gran will be so sad they outlived a grandchild. Gran lost Pappo Jim when I was too young to know him, Dad said burying his dad was so hard and he still missed him after all these years. Dad would talk about Pappo taking him fishing and them spending time quietly relaxing on summer mornings on riverbanks tossing bait in the water.

When dad would take Sara and I fishing he would tell us stories from when he was a boy, maybe taking us girls fishing was a way to keep memories of Pappo alive and share them with us. Sara knew Pappo a bit, she was five or so when he passed, maybe I'll meet Pappo in heaven? Will he recognize me even though he didn't know me? Sara and I weren't good fisher girls, neither of us sat still very long and got bored very quickly and after a few years dad just stopped taking us. I want to be able to fish again.

The paresthesia is beginning to fade, am I losing feeling in my body? I can't feel any throbbing or pain, just an ever frightening dull taking over my body. It feels like my head is slumped forward but I can't feel any of my hair on my face, no blood rushing anywhere, just the booming pressure of a heavy pulse filling my ears. I remember getting my ears pierced a few years ago, they felt hot and flush at first when it happened, that's how my face feels. Mom wanted me to get earrings when I was six or seven but dad said I should be old enough to take care of them myself. I know girls that already have belly rings, at fourteen! What kind of parent wants their daughter showing off body parts and pretending to be older to attract the attention of older boys?

I can't breathe and I feel like I'm getting tired from just trying to catch my breath. Panic is still my company, I can't hear Sara or Katie coughing or screaming, I can't hear cars passing by or engines running, there are no sirens or noises I can distinguish, I only hear the twisting wrecking sounds of the accident; permanently stamped into my ear drums to replay for the rest of my life, however many minutes are left. I'm dying.

What kind of people will read about this accident? What will I be portrayed like? Nowadays the TV is flooded with big-butted wannabe famous people or rich girls with lazy eyes, these girls are only famous because they're famous, no talent and if you chisel away the make-up I bet they are hideous. Tramps with sex tapes and such low IQ's that they don't realize it, and half the girls in my school want to emulate them. Maybe I won't miss that much if I expire tonight.

Maybe I'll be remembered as the cheerful good girl I tried to be, if most of these celebrities died suddenly the world would mourn of course and no one would mention their exploits out of respect, it wouldn't be a week before it would all be "remember that girl who...." And so on. Why am I worrying about stupid adults I'll never know? Ladies that will never have a positive influence on the world but they're latest sex something or drunken stupid something that takes over real news and real interesting life events. Why do people gravel over such media parasites like them?

My body thrust against my seatbelt again. Why does it keep doing that? I don't think the seat is pushing me, am I in a massive car pileup? Oh god what if there are dozens of cars all mashed up and it would take them days to unbind them all and by then be too late for us? Maybe I should stop trying to open my eyes, stop trying to move my arms, stop trying to get a big enough breath to scream.

Do I just give up and slip into the fading emptiness that my body feels? Do I give in and let the cold night air take my last breath from me? Do I succumb to the darkness that shrouds me and dissipate into the nothingness? Is this really what it's like? Do the people that die in their sleep know they die? Do they have dreams of dying and never wake up? What if eternal sleep is really what it is? What if you just dream forever and don't know it? Maybe I'm just dreaming now and can't wake up? Will I suddenly open my eyes and mom will be waking me up, breakfast made and the usual morning rush of before school orchestrated events ready to unfurl before me?

Why can't I wake up? I can remember having dreams of falling or getting hurt and in those dreams things seem to hurt but a bland numbed almost removed type of pain, a pain you know hurts but you can't feel it first hand, this is what it feels like. Maybe I just think things hurt because they're supposed to, like in dreams. Can you think of being in a dream and remembering dreams while in a dream? I am merely a figment of my own imagination.

chapter 3

I THRUST FORWARD but this time I'm lying flat. I can hear a man talking *"Class one MVA trauma, blunt, eta thirty minutes"* what's going on? I can feel tightness across my chest and waist. My body suddenly has sharp pains running through it my neck feels like it is being choked. I can hardly crack my left eye but it's blurry but I see light and things moving. I can't sit up.

"You were in a car accident, you're in an ambulance and you'll be okay," a man's voice said. I felt so glad; I just started crying all over again. I can't sit up and my body is starting to hurt, my legs burn, my right arm feels like it's on fire but I can feel them. I'm not dead! I'm crying so hard, I'm so glad I'm not dead. My whole body feels encased in cement; it's too heavy and won't move. There's music in the background but I can't make it out, some metal noise drowned out by the hollering siren.

I am trying to ask the man where my sister and Katie are but he just keeps telling me *"lay back and relax, you'll be ok"*, where is my mom? I told him my name was Lorna Daniels and my mom Susan should be here somewhere, he reassured me she'll make it to the hospital. He asked me what happened and what I remember. All I could say was that there was a flash of light and then we were hit. I asked him to make the noises stop, my head was pounding and everything hurt. I was so relieved I was alive.

Are Sara and Katie ok? Where is my mom? I'm trying to cry out these questions but the man keeps telling me to lay still and try to relax. Relax? Is this idiot dumb? How am I supposed to relax? My body hurts, I'm strapped down, my head is pounding, I'm being choked, I can't breathe, I have so many questions, feelings, pains and things going on and I can't stop crying. Where are my mom and dad?

There is something on my face, I can feel it across my forehead and over my eyes, I can see underneath it and that loud music and siren are blaring in my head. I can feel the tears streaming down my face and my lungs are still burning with each breath. Is my head bandaged? Am I going to have a giant scar on my face? Was it blood pouring down my face when I had the wet feeling? My shirt still feels wet; did I ruin my camisole and shirt with blood?

My body jerked and jolted again, I can feel the squeeze of something around my neck, straps holding me down around my chest and waist. My legs feel cold and I can feel the cold air on my legs. My legs burn and the pain is thriving in spikes up my back and exploding into my brain. My ears are on fire, it feels like they are pierced again but added with the sense assaulting sirens and some angry voice screaming "FUUEEELLL" on the radio. I want it all to stop, I want quiet again.

Click I awoke to some noise and noticed I'm still strapped into that bed, I can see things swinging and dangling over me under the wrap or cloth that is covering my eyes. I can see blurry images of monitors and hear things beeping. The man at my side keeps calling out numbers like one seventy-four over ninety-six. I don't understand what they are saying but it's oddly comforting to hear something, anything at all. It's hard to focus on anything with the crashing sounds mixed in with that loud awful music and things beeping and the sirens' excruciating noise.

My right arm feels like it's sewn to this still mattress. I can't wiggle my legs or feet. I can't lift my head and there seems to be something wrapped around my neck that is choking me, I want out of this situation. I'm trapped and want to just go home. I miss my bed, I miss my mom, I miss the quiet of the accident earlier, and it's been replaced with this deafening siren.

My body feels so heavy, I can't lift my legs, my arms or even my head, I can't turn and I only have sharp pains everywhere. I can feel the bumps and jumbles of the ambulance, it feels like we're going fast and it's scaring me, I've already been in one accident and I'm terrified we're going to be in another accident. The man notices when I start moving and he just keeps telling me to lay back and relax. If he tells me to relax one more time I'm going to start screaming.

I can't stop crying, I hurt so badly, my chest burns, my belly hurts and I feel like I'm going to throw up. I can feel vomit trying to climb back up my throat. The taste of those concert nachos is coming back to me and I'm starting to regret the second helping. All I can do is try to focus on not throwing up, how would I throw up? I'd have to puke on myself since I'm strapped down and can't move. I can't stop crying enough to moan and my head is killing me.

I can't focus, my head is spinning, I'm woozy and my stomach feels full and heavy and this may not end well. How long till we get to the hospital? How far have we driven? Why am I still shaking? My legs are cold; my face feels hot and puffy. I had poison ivy once when I was younger and my face was so swollen it stung just as much as it itched, my face itches now as much as it hurts. I feel hot and cold.

Things in my body sting and burn, I'm miserable. My eyes burn and won't stop leaking tears. My chest burns with each labored breath and the straps that have me tied down constrict with each attempt to move. I keep feeling the shaking of the ambulance through the bed thing I'm fastened to, reassuring me parts of me are still attached. I feel like I have been rolled in glass.

Each bump on the road in the ambulance feels like being in mini accidents, the jostle of the straps burn and press on my body in areas that hurt each time, I feel like I'm swelling into the straps like a tree that has overgrown onto a fence post. The straps feel like they're cutting into me. The pressure within me makes me feel like that cartoon cat that swallowed dynamite and has exploded inside. I need to vomit.

My head is pounding, my throat is spasming, and my stomach is trying to violently empty itself. ARRGHHHSSHHHH, I feel a little better but I just vomited all over myself. I can't tell where everything landed but the pressure relief inside of me feels better. I don't know if I hit the medic guy or myself or any of the equipment or just all of it. My eyes feel heavy again, I'm so dizzy.

I can feel myself fading in and out. I woke up again and things keep flooding back to me, the light veering into our car, the flash before the screeching hell of noise and the symphony of twisting steel, glass screams and terror howls of your sister and good friend in the front seat. My body started shaking again; I feel the jolt of pain writhing through me causing me to cry again. My legs burn and the pain shooting up through my chest and into my neck then head. I can only taste the blood and vomit in my mouth; I can't smell anything but my chest still burns with that chemical that filled it.

How long till I get to the hospital? This trip seems to go on forever. Where is Sara? Katie? Are they ok? Where is my mom? *"My name is Walker and you'll be ok"*. The voice nearest to me introduced himself. He had an odd voice but it was nice to hear anything besides that screaming siren and whatever grunge noise that resembled that twisting crunching sound of the accident.

My eyes and throat burn with that taste of the chemical that burned in that accident. My body still shook and my bare legs were freezing. I felt my whole body shiver as I cried. The straps were constricting tighter and tighter, I couldn't just lay here, I was crying, my legs burned, I was covered in nacho vomit and I hurt all over, I smelled awful.

My legs were on fire and the pain thrashed into my pelvis and through to my chest, each pounding heart beat delivered ambushing pain that made me shake as I sobbed. How long am I supposed to endure this pain? My body jerked and jolted against the straps and each time they seemed to crush harder onto me. The chest strap squeezed tighter and tighter and the strap around my waist felt like it was going to cut me into two like some sadistic magician.

Will I ever walk again? I can't feel my feet, my legs throb and burn and the throbbing feels like it's taking over my whole body. Each bump in the road as we drove seemed to heave me against those burdensome straps. The echoing siren overthrew any thoughts I tried to have, I tried to think about running through wild flowers or tall grasses in the spring with my hands outstretched feeling the tips running through my fingers.

I loved the spring, once the rotten smell of thawed winter faded and the sweet air came in from Lake Michigan and April set in. April led to warm afternoons with cool evenings but the days got longer and the magic Michigan flip came. The magic Michigan flip was funny, at sixty degrees in October people tucked into thick coats and hoodies while sixty degrees in the spring meant people were sporting short shorts and tank tops. It was a funny irony, but heavy long winters that spread cabin fever and seasonal mood disorder, or just depressed people enough to keep huddled indoors for months.

I loved sledding and building snowmen with Sara, will that ever happen again? Is Sara ok? I wish I knew how she was, I miss her and I'm so scared. Will I ever walk again? I can feel myself fading in and out and each time I jolt awake my body throbs in searing burning pain. The machines beeping in this ambulance is maddening. My chest burns and keeps feeling tighter and tighter. I can't breathe and crying keeps making me more and more tired.

I'm so tired. Could this be the spiral to dying? What if I just get so tired and keep closing my eyes. I'm tired of trying to stay awake, what if I just fall asleep and never wake up? My heart throbbing and pounding in my head is almost in rhythm with that evil music in the background that is fighting for dominance of sound in my ears.

Click "squish squish squish" I can feel something squeezing on my left arm, it's so tight. "One eighty over ninety-five" Walker shouted to the driver. There is so much going on, I can't focus, and it's overbearing my mind with so much going on. The beeps, the whoo whoo erghh werghh is so loud in my ears but I keep reimagining that flash then the thrashing crashing twisting metal crunching of the accident.

I remember having Katie, Ryann, and their dad Mr. Matt over for thanksgiving. We had a big turducken, it's a turkey that has a chicken crammed inside it with a duck shoved inside of that, and it was oh so yummy. Of course dad and Mr. Matt spoke about rebuilding that mustang, C4 transmission and a 289 engine, whatever that means. Katie, Sara and I played dance superstar and Ryann just read the latest National Geographic magazine and sat quietly on the couch. Ryann was a quiet guy and one of those nerdy kinds of guys that sat in his basement room. He worked at a pizza place most afternoons so he wasn't around much but Katie said he was always intrigued with archaeology and old societies.

Ryann was always trying to encourage Katie to take interest in cultures that have died out hundreds or thousands of years ago. Oh god, will his interest in dead things include me? Am I going to die still? How often do people die in ambulances? I thought this was the carriage that would deliver me safely to a hospital and I'll be ok. What if the chest strap keeping me in this bed, crush me to death? What if I just don't wake up?

Katie and Ryann's mom left their dad Mr. Matt when Katie was nine. Ms. Ellen and Mr. Jerry, the Matts, seemed to work a lot as they fell apart. Upside was, after their divorce they moved in a few houses down and that's when Sara and Katie started spending a lot of time together. I have a lot of memories of summers of Sara and Katie spending time with me. I got to tag along whenever they went to Dairy Queen or the park. We had so many summers of kite flying and swinging. I hope Katie is alright.

I can barely see under a crack of my left eye, my right eye is too heavy to open and it hurts too much to try to open. I can feel tears trickling down my face and into my ear muffling the sounds of my ambulance. Things sound gurgly and waterlogged. I saw an orange beat up looking cell phone swipe in then out of my vision. Things keep getting blurry as my eye wells up with a tear; before it fills my eye just before tipping out of the corner then down my cheekbone.

What will be said at my eulogy? Will mom and dad know how I felt about them? Will they play some sad song or each person say their fondest memory about me? Is my life just over? Why do some people get eighty or ninety years and get to start and have giant wonderful families that gather around generations during the holidays and I'm going to die at fourteen? How is life fair that when my family gathers for holidays I won't be there ever again? Are my last words to my mom through a text? The impersonal text messaging, not voices over the phone, not the comforting sounds of hearing her voice that has warmed my heart forever.

I want my mommy, I want her here telling me that things will be ok, I want her running her fingers through my hair like she did when I was sick and stayed home with me to keep me company. In fifth grade I got sick with a terrible stomach ache and I slept the entire day with my head on her lap and she stroked my hair. I wish my head was in her lap and I wasn't in this ambulance and I wish this night never happened. I miss my mom.

I miss the low key days of lounging around the house, Saturdays that started off with Hillshire farms sausage links and pancakes then meld into cartoons or yard work with Sara and mom. I wish I was only sick and dealing with little things that would pass in a day or two. I'm scared and alone and I can't even see this voice next to me that just keeps rambling numbers.

How long am I trapped in this limb strapped to a bed that shakes and assaults my already battered body? I am too small and my little body hurts more than it can handle. I can't stop crying or shaking, I'm freezing. My heart is throbbing and each pulse makes my neck expand against this collar that's choking me and making it hard to swallow. My nose is clogged and my head is pounding. I can't breathe and everything is tightening on me.

My body is heavy and nothing moves. My right side is swelling and I can't feel my hands or feet. I can only feel pain shooting from my legs, my thighs feel like I ran for a month straight, my adrenaline is running and everything feels like slow motion. Each wail of the siren is blaring slowly and sharp in my ears. My left ear is muffled and gargling because it is full of my tears and my right ear feels hot. My face feels heavy and this cloth on my head feels wet and feels like it's pinning me down. I'm immobile and feel like I'm glued to a board, I'm imprisoned.

I remember being at Millpond Park last summer with Sara, we were swinging and waiting for Katie to finish with her acting seminar at school and we walked past the play structure and we saw a snake. The snake was a small garter but holy smokes, Sara shrieked so loud and we couldn't run fast enough to get away from it. When we reached the swing we stood on it to make sure it wasn't slithering towards us trying to attack us. We tried to retell the story to Katie when she met up with us but we were laughing so hard we couldn't keep motion on the swings. We were such dorks.

Kelly was into reading, she enjoyed books like "The House of Six" and "3rd hand Ranch" she enjoyed reading a lot but was also a cross country runner with Sara and also into plays with Katie. She was also a thin brunette but couldn't sing like Katie. Kelly was very popular and outgoing. She didn't get to play with us as much because she was so busy but she was so funny. One time flying kites she was running all over trying to get her kite to crash into ours, Sara got so mad that her pink and black kite went tumbling down because Kelly got her kite to ram it.

Kelly was the middle child of three, she had bookend brothers is what she called them, and was a bit of a tomboy. She was elegant and had a smooth walk about her but was always cheerful and funny. Kelly loved laughing and playing pranks. Once at Millpond she grabbed one of those baby garter snakes and hid it in her pocket, of course at the right time the pulled it out and Sara must have peed her pants, and tripped on herself trying to run and fell. Katie scurried for some distance and plowed me right over. We ended up laughing hysterically while Kelly spoke like a baby to comfort that squirming little reptile. We laughed at Kelly cause she was so calm, but she laughed at the three of us for freaking out over a tiny shoelace sized snake.

We had plans to bring fishing gear to the park. Each time we had plans to fish like dad took us out doing, we would chicken out and purposely forget poles or gear because honestly; none of us wanted to unhook a fish, they were slimy. Kelly's oldest brother Brandon was kind of cute but being a senior he had other interests than spending time with her. Her younger brother Mikey was an annoying ten year old and was always being a pest. Mikey loved pulling her hair or taking her bras from the dryer and used them as G.I Joe catapults. Brothers can be irritating but some of the things he came up with were pretty funny.

Kelly and Katie were in a school play of Peter Pan last year for their spring sing thing at school. It was funny because they were both in competition of who could text Sara more while on stage. There was a big fake rock onstage that they ducked behind as lost boys and they were texting Sara, while Sara and I sat in the audience. Kelly won with ninety three to Katie's' eighty four. Those girls were crazy. What is Kelly going to think when she hears what happened?

I wish it wasn't me strapped down. I wish it wasn't me freezing and in pain enduring this onslaught of hell. What if Kelly was able to go to the concert and I was in bed by now. What if Kelly was riding in the back seat and I wouldn't have this frightful image of the headlight charging into the passenger door or the thrashing metal or glass screams in her head instead of mine.

I can't keep the screaming of tires or sounds of glass screams out of my head. The twisting shrieking metal encapsulating us as it wraps around the highway divider over and over. I can't focus on anything but the shearing pain in my legs and my entire right side is throbbing with each heartbeat.

My head is spinning and pounding. The wailing siren is keeping me from try-ing to sleep, I'm so tired. I can't seem to stop crying but I don't feel tears running down my face anymore. I writhe and hurt with each bump as we make our way to the hospital.

I'm so scared. Where is my mom? Did anyone call her? How will she know where I am? How is Katie or Sara? Are they OK? How long until we're at the hospital? Was it going to be like a TV show with doctors scurrying about, shouting things like "stat" and hollering at nurses to move faster and organized chaos turning out lifesaving events? Each bump in the road shakes this bed I'm strapped to and my body jolts and the collar on my neck pushes against my collar bones.

This collar is choking me. My body hurts and shooting pains grow and pulse up from my legs, there's pressure on my stomach and pelvis. My right side is tingling and things throb within me. I can't stop crying and I'm scared and trying not to panic. I should be ok now that I'm in an ambulance. I feel better being here rather than entombed in that mangled coffin smell-ing chemicals and burning things. I want to be in my bed.

Is mom or dad going to be at the hospital waiting for me? Do they know what happened? Did someone find their numbers in my phone? I should have texted them, I wish I could have found my phone and used it to call them. My body keeps trembling and writhing in pain, the pain shoots through me and over takes me, I can't control it.

The voice next to me keeps telling me to lay back and relax and that everything will be ok. The sounds of the glass shattering in my ears moan in and out with the cries of the siren and that terrible noise on the radio. I hear the driver call out things to a radio like "eta..." and "enroot" and I hope it means we're close.

I asked Walker, the voice close to me, if he knew how Sara and Katie were, did they make it? Are they going to be at the hospital also? Walker said the helicopter took the front passenger, Katie, and another, the driver, but he didn't know any other answers. Walker said there was a big truck that plowed into us and we'll be at the hospital soon.

Walker kept telling me to lay back and relax. I kept hearing snapping sounds and under the cloth on my face I see flashes of a cell phone, things swinging in the air then things blur out with tears. I see lines and tube things and I keep shaking and the bumps make the straps around me keep squeez-ing tighter and tighter around me. I can't tell if I have to pee or the pain in my belly is just trying to explode.

My legs don't work. Another jolt climbs to my chest from my legs. My right arm feels like cement, the tingling from my legs to my feet make my heart pound in my head. My neck pulses against the collar and it seems to clinch tighter and tighter, will this thing kill me? Is there still a chance I might die? Will I have to have surgery? What if they cut off something or I can't ever use my arms or legs again? I want to go running with Sara. Will Kelly feel bad that she could have been in my position but missed it with slim karma? Where is my mommy? I want her here stroking my hair and whispering that I'll be ok.

I want be at home, in my pink room covered in my band collages with my radio on and my parents down stairs not more than two seconds away. I want to be in the garage watching my dad toil on the mustang he loves and talking about taking us girls to the Woodward dream cruise and checking out all the other cars. I want to be out of this chamber that's strangling me and keeping me prisoner. The beeping and noises of the sirens are making my headache worse. My eyes feel dry and it's getting hard to open them.

The things swinging in my limited vision are making me dizzy. The cloth on my face seems like its falling and going to suffocate me. I don't like things on my face; my make-up is probably all over the place. Mom didn't like much make-up; dad was against it whole heartedly. Dad squirmed when I started shaving my legs but mom explained it was part of life and at thirteen I was becoming more aware of myself. Dad wriggled last summer when we were shopping at Meijer and I saw this super cute top and the look on his face was a mix of horror or that of having smelled something mildly toxic.

Dad loved having girls but I'm sure deep down he also wanted a boy. Dad fought the idea of his baby girls growing up and becoming women. I hope we'll get through this crap. What would happen if both of his girls died? What would happen if Sara and I both died? Is she ok? How long is this ambulance ride? My head feels heavy and I'm dizzy and feel like I'm going to be sick again.

I jolt back awake again. I lurch against the straps on my chest and waist. My legs feel like they're flopping all over. Would Kelly cry all summer, would she know how much she made us laugh and miss us as much as she'd be missed if she were gone? What is happening to Katie or Sara? Why did they put Katie on the helicopter? Will she be ok too? Did anyone else throw up all over themselves? What if I get to the hospital and I have to wait any longer? How long will I be in the hospital? Will I be mangled or crippled or how long will it be until I'm back to my life and back in school?

My eyes blurt open again. I'm trying to focus on that swinging thing; it's a bag that has a tube running to it. Is Walker texting? I keep seeing his hand holding his phone swoop in and out of my view. Who the hell is he to text? What is he thinking? Isn't there something he should be doing? Fix me or something you idiot. Are we close? I'm trying to ask him how much longer but I can't seem to come up with words, I sound like I'm murmuring and weeping.

I'm getting tired again. My adrenaline is pulsing and running like I've run downhill full speed and can't stop. Yawning hurts all over. My lungs feel like I'm being sat on and trying to open my mouth to yawn is inhibited by this collar and my beating heart to so hard and against this collar and it feels like one of the vice things dad uses to hold pipes to work on.

What time is it? How long has it been since we left the concert? Is mom aware that we should have been home by now? Is she worrying and she and dad calling hospitals to find us? What hospital am I going to? What happened to the drivers of the truck? What caused the accident? Why did this have to happen to me? That concert was so awesome and things were so awesome tonight, why did this have to happen?

What did mom and dad do for dinner tonight? An empty house and no girls to cook for, did they have a date night and enjoy the quiet house or sit back and watch a movie? Did dad duck away to work on the mustang and mom to work on a puzzle? Why is my mind wandering so much? Why does my body hurt so much? What are the doctors going to do? Am I going to die alone? Are my mom and dad going to make it to the hospital and be by my side? Am I being selfish that I want both of my parents by my side and forget about Sara? What if Sara dies? Oh my god I don't want my sister to die!!!

I want Katie and Sara to be at the hospital waiting for me and for them to be ok and I'm getting tired and I want to just go to sleep and wake up in my bed. I want to go home. My pounding heart is slowing a little, my head is so heavy. I'm cold and shivering. Even with my eyes closed I see the light shining through letting in that light red through my eyelids.

chapter 4

"Slam" I feel the car stop abruptly and now there's a commotion, I hear all new voices shouting. "13 year old female, MVA, prolonged extrication" I heard Walker say. I see strobes of light under the rag on my eyes. I see ceiling tiles and florescent lights alternate as I rolled under them. The dizziness is getting worse and my headache is pounding behind my eyes. People shouting and words I don't recognize are being used.

I see a giant bright light swinging over my head. I feel cold all over. I feel those vice straps release and poking and prodding. I feel someone tugging at my feet and someone shaking my hands. Different people keep asking me questions like; "what's your name? Do you know where you are? How old are you? Is there a chance you're pregnant?" I feel colder and the slight breezes feel like they're covering me all over. *"Pregnant?"* I haven't even kissed a boy.

I hear fabric tearing and it feels like they're cutting off my skirt. Oh god I'm half naked and I'm surrounded by tons of people. A bright flash swoops across my eyes. I can't see anything but spots. The doctors said I was in a car accident, and have sustained some trauma. I'm not sure what he means by trauma, is something wrong? How long till I'm better?

The doctor guy said something about a C.T. there was a nurse that warned me they are going to put in a catheter, I didn't know what that meant but I felt a really **REALLY** bad pain in my downstairs, it feels like I was stabbed down there with a turkey baster, it hurts so bad. I feel hands on my chest, is this normal? Why the hell are they feeling my chest? I hardly have breasts and the last summer when they started showing up, my skin itched something fierce, breasts are terrible.

I know my body has been changing and mom and Sara warned me about the changing and fun pains of puberty. I've only had a few periods and they have been a surprise each time. The "monthly" visit has been sporadic and very untimely. I don't like being a girl with this crap. Pads give me an awful rash but I'm too scared to use a tampon and I don't like the idea.

This emergency room has so much going on. There's tons of hustle and bustle, it's overwhelming and confusing. I'm still scared and I don't see my mom or dad. I don't want my dad to see me lying here naked. Why are these strangers keeping me here without my clothes on? I don't like being cold or naked, exposed to the staff. How many people are looking at my naked body? I want to cover up but I can't move my arms. I looked to my left arm and watched someone shove a large needle into it, right in the inner elbow fold and now I can't bend that elbow either. They half covered me with a sheet but I'm still freezing.

Men are looking all over my uncovered unclad body. These guys are wearing scrubs so I assume they belong here but why are they checking me out? What role do they play and what purpose are they looking at me, so very intimately? I don't want to be exposed and naked; I want to be at home. I just want to cry. I feel like I have to pee. All the lights and people talking and people putting things on me and movements going on are making me dizzy, I feel sick.

My heart is pounding again, the surge of adrenaline is spiking again and I feel my heart pounding against my chest wall and my neck keeps bumping against the collar around my neck. I can't swallow, I feel like I have a mouth full of glass like my throat is filling with glass and blood again. I feel like I'm choking and it hurts to swallow.

I had my braces taken off last summer and I remember licking my teeth to feel how smooth they felt after two years of being in pain from the barb wire like brackets they use. The first few months of the wires and brackets hurt so badly, it feels like I have a mouth full of those brackets and my whole body still hurts. Where is my mom? How long till she's here? Did someone call her? Why is there a hose in my lady parts? Why won't my arm move? What's happening and what's going on?

The doctor told me he's sending me to CAT scan to check for internal bleeding. What does that mean? Am I going to bleed to death inside? They wheeled me into a smaller room; there was a giant machine in there with a hole in the middle. They lifted me off one bed and onto another freezing table for the scan. They warned me that they were going to put a contrast inside of me to see better. The contrast stuff made my mouth taste funny, like I had licked a battery. One time when I was younger my dad convinced me to touch my tongue to a 9 volt battery and the buzz was unexpected and the after taste was so gross.

I got off the table and went back to the emergency room. Things were still a busy mess but I didn't hear anything about Katie or Sara. Where were they? Are they alive, ok or what? I'm still covered in a sheet and then more doctors came to talk to me. The red haired lady who looked like she's had a long day introduced herself as the trauma doctor and said I need to go to surgery. "Surgery??" She said I had bilateral breaks in my legs and they need to pin things.

I laid there freezing in that bed. The bed sheets under me were warming up but I felt wet. I could feel my hair was a mess, I had it combed and straightened earlier in the evening, and I was so cute and ready to spend the evening with my sister and our friend. The concert was so awesome. Why did this have to happen?

I kept trying to think about the concert, the swaying cowgirls dressed up all cute and sexy. The cowboy hats on all the rugged cowboys, the thundering speakers and the laughs among us girls. I keep trying to close my eyes and focus on the concert and block off all the beeping and people running around. There are nurses stabbing me with needles, carts full of drawers and people rummaging through them. I feel like a pin cushion, I have guys and girls putting things on me, in me, and I don't know what's going on, I just can't stop crying.

I jolt again, my body hurts and the pain from my legs travel up my pelvis, through my belly, it feels like my heart is going to explode. "Get this collar off of me" I shouted. My face feels sticky and I smell like vomit. I feel like the pillow is sticking to me. I looked to my right, there is a stand full of cords and machines and suddenly there was a tall guy, he was wearing a paper hat and looked like he hadn't shaved or slept in a week, he said he was a surgeon and was going to take me upstairs. The surgeon had two girls with him, one in a cute blonde ponytail the other a brunette with her hair in one of those blue hairnet things. Those doctors said it'll be a few minutes.

The surgeons explained that they also found that I had some bleeding inside and that they'll have to open me up and stitch the spot inside, I asked if they found my parents yet. They told me that they are waiting for my parents to sign consent to allow them to operate but that I had to sign a paper just in case. What happened to Katie or Sara? I'm so hungry. There is a nurse sitting by my legs, she keeps writing things down but hardly looking at me.

The nurse at the foot just kept writing things down, I tried to clear my throat and crackle "what's going on?" she hardly looked at me and just told me that I was in a car accident. I understand I was in an accident but I have so many more questions; where are my parents? What's wrong with me? How much longer am I stuck here? Where is Sara? Are mom and dad with her? I told her that my parents were James and Susan Daniels and they need to be called. The nurse told me she has people trying to call them.

The nurse didn't leave my side although she barely spoke. I felt comfortable that she was there but cold and distant because I didn't even know her name or what the hell she was doing. My anxiety is starting to flare up and not knowing what's going on is starting to get to me. I need to know what's going on, what's happening to Sara or Katie and why don't they know? What hospital did they go to? The nurse said she'd call and find out where they went but for now she had to keep monitoring my vital signs.

What are vital signs? I can feel pain in my body, I can't move anything still. I am naked, hardly covered by a sheet, I feel like a sticker board with all the patch things on my body, I'm full of needles and tubes and they keep taking blood from me but keep hooking up IV bags to refill me. I'm still dizzy and my head is thumping with my heart pounding in my ears. I can feel the sheet against my skin, why is it still cold? I don't want to have surgery, I'm a young fit girl, I think I'm attractive, I don't want my body cut up or scarred.

I want to get out of here. I want to go to sleep, I'm exhausted. My eyelids are so heavy, I can't keep them open. My chest still burns and it's hard to breathe, every inhale hurts and it feels like I'm still being squeezed. My mind is wandering and my head spinning, I feel like most of the chaos that is charging this place is in my brain. It feels like there's a giant behind my eyes trying to kick them out of my head, it's like they want to explode.

I still can't figure out what happened tonight. It went from an awesome amazing time and even as the evening began to wind down and the trip home commenced. I never imagined this could have happened. The glass screams keep echoing through my mind. The flash of lights that transpired the series of tonight's events seemed to be burned into my eyes, even when they are closed I can't stop seeing them. Is Katie ok? She was in front. Where is my mom?

My mind keeps going back and envisioning the spidering of the glass breaking and then being pelted with glass shards. I can feel pricks of glass in my head as I lay here. The burning smell of the car has permanently taken over any smell of this hospital. I remember being in one when I twisted my ankle running last year. That hospital smelled like disinfectant and sterile smells, this one smells like burning chemicals. There are so many people standing around me, I don't like so many people around when I'm laying here unclothed.

I can feel the sheet against my body. My chest feels like the sheet is crushing me and I can't breathe. My stomach hurts. This tube sticking in my parts hurts so bad, this thing feels like it's shoved into me so far it's hurting to breathe. I don't know what's going on around here. What's happening to me?

The surgeons are still standing around, what are they waiting for? Why do they keep staring at me? Is the nurse over at the foot of the bed going to do anything? The nurse keeps looking at the monitors above me and back at her clipboard but keeps avoiding eye contact with me. My anxiety is acting up, I'm super nervous and freaking out again. My pulse is racing again and my head is pounding like the drums from the concert a few hours ago.

I remember from biology that red blood cells carry oxygen all over the body; I also remember that blood accumulates in areas of injury causing bruises. It feels like my whole body is bruising and swollen. I feel like I won't ever fit into my clothes again. I was so petite and thin and I feel like all the fluids that are running into my arms are filling my legs.

I feel like my legs have turned to tree trunks but they're on fire. My whole body throbs with each heart beat and my head pounds and my eyes throb along with my legs. My whole body seems to pulse with each hard thud of my heart. I want to go home and watch gossip shows with mom. Where is my mom at? Where are Sara and Katie? Are they OK? Why doesn't anybody do anything? Why doesn't anyone know anything?

I asked the nurse at the end of the bed if she has any more information about my sisters. She doesn't even tell me no she just shakes her head, does this lady even care? Did they die? Am I ever going to kiss a boy? Is any boy ever going to want to date me if I'm disfigured or am I going to have to live with my parents for the rest of my life? How long am I going to live? Are the doctors just going to wait for me to die here so some doctor doesn't have a death to ruin his record or operating statistics? Am I just going to fall asleep and never wake up?

I'm so tired. I feel like my body is going numb and I'm too tired to keep fighting to stay awake. It's getting too hard to keep breathing. These tubes in my nose itch and I feel like my nose is running. The nurse at the end of the bed just stands there. My body lunges and lurches feel weaker each time. My pulse feels like it's starting to slow down. Am I falling asleep or dying?

I'm still so scared. I can feel my eyes water with tears again. My legs and arms are starting to go numb. The pain in me is starting to numb over and I'm so tired. Am I going to die in this hospital? I want my mom and dad. Where are Katie and Sara? What time is it? How long was I in the ambulance? Why was I seeing that guy's cell phone? There is so much in my head and it's all so jumbled and racing.

There is a tickle in my throat and I can't get a big enough breath to cough. My chest is tight and I can't breathe. I lay here with my body going to sleep but and my mind struggling to fight it. I wonder why I see so many people die on the news, is it worth it? All these stupid people fighting, killing each other over stupid crap but for no real reason at all. My mom would be so disappointed that I swore. I wonder if the people that died regretted what they were dying for. Life is so precious and short, I'm only fourteen and that's all I'll have.

I don't like casseroles and I don't like peas but there isn't anything I hate. I have never felt hate in my heart. I don't understand how people can get to a point that they hate, let alone hate enough to kill someone. I may be young and naïve and have only known love in my life and it's been a beautiful life. I've enjoyed loving parents, bright warm sun, letting my hair flow behind me as I ran or rode with the window open driving down the road. I've loved, loved home cooking, beautiful music, music that inspires and lifts your heart, so many things.

I've felt warming, caring, nurturing that I imagine all parents want for their children. Sara and I have been blessed and had both dreamt of having our own kids and sharing stories of our childhood. Childhood, I'm hardly a teenager and I look at these past few years as a childhood like it's over and I'm ready to be a mother myself. Am I supposed to wait for the infamous bright light or tunnel or warming calming white? Am I going to know I'm dying while I'm dying or am I dying and not knowing it? Am I still trapped in the car and my mind has concocted all of this in some philosophical way where things mean all sorts of other things?

I wanted to go to a big college with giant oak trees and people laid out underneath them studying. I want to attend a college that offers a real education and isn't hung up on its prestige and looks. I want to be one of those cute girls hugging her books as she scuffles down walk ways in cool fall days like the magazine articles I've thumbed through. I want professors dressed in classy tweed that look over their glasses perched on the end of their nose as they address large classes.

I've spent this last school year figuring out that most of these formative years are just a matter of surviving then the real education and life lessons are learned out and on your own. I want a dorm with other girls of substance not the slutty ones that seem to infest cable TV. I once heard that MTV played actual music and not hog slop that oozes across the screen. I don't understand how so many girls are so shallow and quick to give away their love. True love has always been special to me.

My view of true love is that of my parents, yuck I know. Love is the wanting to be there in the morning after a fight, the strength to be you and not hide insecurities. Love is the relief of being yourself and to laugh and also aim to be what you see in the lovey dovey movies at the same time. One time mom laughed at the room full of rose's thing on a movie and dad did it anyways and the hug they shared was awesome. Sara and I always oohed and awed at them to poke fun but knew that's what we aimed for in our future husbands. Katie always hung around and oodled over what mom and dad had, hoping for the same thing in her future also.

Girls at school were in a hurry to skank up like the overweight or lazy eyed rich hoochies on TV. I don't like the cliques that are spiraling toward slutsville, they all encourage each other to out tramp each other just like the bimbo's on the reality channels. I am baffled at what kinds of parents' raise these girls; I assume they are on cue with the same parents that produce strippers, just with a financial background. Heiress or not you still have a lazy eye and poor taste. Dogs are also meant to be walked not carried, superficial girls disgusted me.

Oh my head hurts, I can still feel my heart pounding but it's getting as weak as I am. I wanted so many adventures in my life, I want to take a trip and backpack though Europe to see cathedrals and paintings worth more than I could ever count. I want to see paintings that have been painted long before this country was ever claimed. I want to smell the same smells that people have smelled thousands of years ago in caves and churches. I want to see the birth place of sciences and religions side by side.

So many of these TV girls have so many abilities at their fingertips to travel and explore like pilgrims of long ago but spend it drinking and partying with guys that think they have too much to offer but couldn't muster eight brain cells. It's a shame that so much potential knowledge is passed on just because mommy and daddy have money or they've made a slut tape. I miss my cute undies and comfy flannel pajamas; I don't want to be sitting here naked.

How long have I been laying here. I can hear a clock above me and its ticking is maddening but I can't see it. I can't move my head enough to try to glimpse a reflection of someone's watch as so many people run around like a flock of geese. I miss my bed; I miss my comforter that I wrap around me to snuggle in warmly with my feet jutting out of the bottom. Mom always laughed that even on summer nights I roll up snuggly but keep my feet out of the bottom to keep me from getting too hot. I'm more comfortable with my feet dangling out of the bottom.

My eyes are so heavy, they feel like they are sticking closed but keep leaking, am I full of this fluid and its pouring out of my eyes? This stupid tube in my nose tickles so badly and my nose feels like it's full of boogs and I can't move my arms to do anything about it. God I couldn't pick my nose in here, it's not lady like. I want to shower, I feel the vomit on me and it's so gross. My god some of these young doctor guys have seen my body and can see me in such a shamble, I'm a gross mess.

I can't get comfortable, there is glass stabbing my head and I feel like I'm cemented to this stretcher. Where is my mom? Where is my dad? Am I dying? What happened to Sara or Katie? Why isn't anyone doing anything, I thought I was going to be operated on? Why are people standing around and picking their butts?

chapter 5

MY EYES ARE heavy and I can't open them anymore. I feel like I'm moving, there was a thump of the bed and my head feels like it's swaying when they turn me. I hear a few voices talking to each other, one says they'll open my belly to stop some internal bleeding and after they "close" they'll work that leg pinning thing. "Lorna" I hear a voice call my name, it sounds like that trauma lady from earlier, and "we're taking you to surgery" she warns me.

The lady voice warns me that the surgery may take a few hours but I won't feel a thing and I'll be much better when I wake up. My body feels like a water balloon, it feels like my skin is being stretched and I jiggle as I hit bumps in the hallway. My lower back feels sore and my butt hurts too. I still feel like I'm numb, the good part is there aren't sharp pains anymore but why am I getting numb? Am I dying or falling asleep. I'm so tired. Where are my parents?

I felt like I was swung backwards, then more thumps on the stretcher. I hear voices hovering over me and, they are talking about cutting me and something about mesenteric something. I feel a dull pressure on my stomach, it feels like I'm being poked or something. I don't have the strength to open my eyes. I'm so sleepy and I want to go home. I want to be with my parents and be left alone.

I feel throbs and pains in my head; someone lifted my head for a minute. A guy's voice tells me that we're headed back. I feel the thumps of the stretcher again and it feels like we're moving again. My head bobs and rolls as we turn corners. I'm cold again. I can feel my body shivering, the sheet on me is still cold and I feel like I'm getting even more numb. My eyes throb with my heart beat, the stretcher thumps again. I hear many more voices and murmuring. It sounds like metal clinging and clanging all around me, more machines making beeping noises, and plastic ripping. What's going on?

I feel my anxiety climbing again. My heart is starting to race and a machine is starting to beep louder and faster which is making me more nervous. What is the beeping? Someone touched my eyes and now someone is messing with my mouth. What the heck is going on? Someone whispers to me that it's time to go to sleep. It's about time, I'm so tired.

Mommy? I hear a lady's voice talking to me. "No sweetheart my name is Janet" I feel my eyes watering again. I'm so sleepy and tired and just want to go home. Janet tells me I'm in recovery, what kind of recovery? I hear two men talking, Janet tells me "Mike" is her other recovery nurse and she needs me to open my eyes. I can't, they feel so heavy. I just want to go to sleep and then wake up when this nightmare is over. Why can't I just wake up in my bed, at home, mom making breakfast, dad hollering that the sports section is wet. I miss my parents, my home, and my sister.

A man's voice pipes up and introduces himself, "I'm Mike and I'll be helping Janet take care of you" he tells me that the surgery is over and the Doctor is on her way to see me. A lady doctor is pretty cool. The lady doctors' voice from before takes over, she tells me that the internal bleeding was controlled, the surgery took a few hours and I'll be in the hospital for a while. Why is she telling me this? Where are my parents?

Mike says I have a visitor, Dad is here. "Daddy?" I shouted. I'm crying again, this time I'm crying harder than before and I'm so relieved he's here. "Sweetpea its daddy" I hear my dad's voice. I can hardly open my eyes but they do open and the tears are streaming down both sides of my face. I see my legs lifted up and wrapped in bandages. I see a stocky man with a white goatee and a lady with a short bob haircut and glasses, and my dad. Dad rushes to my side, sits on the bed and hugs me tighter than I can ever remember him hugging me before.

I can feel my body writhing with my crying. I'm so scared, happy, overwhelmed, my emotions have overtaken me. My dad's big strong arms are under me and lifting me to him, and he down to me. I feel his hands so softly stroking my hair like he had when I was little. My legs hurt and I'm still so tired but I don't want to go to sleep. I'm afraid to wake up and dad not be here. Dad shushes me and tells me he's not leaving me or going anywhere.

My eyes close again and sleep has overtaken me. I wake up to the beeping of more machines behind me. The room is light and I feel daylight cracking through the blinds. Dad is asleep in the chair next to me with his feet up on the bed. "Daddy?" he responds telling me he's here and that I'm ok. Where is Mom? Sara? What happened?

Dad tells me that mom is at another hospital with Sara but that she's alive. Oh thank god she's alive. Why are we at different hospitals? What happened? I can feel myself crying again. Is Katie ok? Dad starts crying, crying! I've never seen him cry before. This scares me so bad, why is he crying? Dad told me that he and mom had both of us.

Dad told me the cops found my phone in the car and answered it as he was calling for the nine hundredth time since they hadn't heard from us. Mom was calling Sara's phone and dad mine. Dad rushed to my hospital and mom to Sara's. There was a state trooper at each hospital to meet a parent, he and mom had to show the cops pictures of us to help identify us since our purses had been in the car.

Sara was flown to a larger hospital because she was in worse shape. Mom was scared and crying but her strong mom instincts took over and she drove to see Sara while dad rushed to be by my side. Dad had texted mom a lot over night to keep up with Sara's condition. Dad was still crying, he said he was so glad his girls were ok. Dad cleared his throat really hard, blew his nose then looked at me with sadness in his heart.

"*Katie didn't make it*" he said. "NOOO" I cried out, dad started crying again. He said Katie and Sara were at the same hospital because they both got in the same helicopter. Mom picked up Mr. Matt and they both drove to Sara's hospital. Dad told me Katie didn't even make it to the hospital. Sara was pinned in the car and in pretty bad shape but the steering wheel kept her from being crushed. Katie was hit bluntly and passed away shortly after being freed from the wreck.

At least she didn't die in the accident, just as a result of it. He proceeded to tell me it looked like the truck hit some black ice and veered right into Katie's door. If the angle had been any less then Sara wouldn't be here with us he said. I can't stop crying, why Katie? She was my other sister. The crackle of the glass screams echoed in my mind, suddenly I was back in the accident and all I can hear is Katie crying.

My heart is racing, thumping and pounding in my chest, it's hard to swallow, I can't breathe, I don't know if I can cry any harder but I want to. "Dad; can you make it all better?" I asked, Dad is crying as hard as I am. I'm getting tired again; my head is starting to spin. The nurse comes in and tells me that I should try to rest as she puts that squeezy thing on my arm and looks under my sheet.

"Pumpkin" I wake back up to dad's voice. I'm still in this stupid hospital, and I'm still freezing under this measly sheet. "It's midday and you should try to eat" he tells me. There is a tray on a table cart thing next to me. I can't eat, I'm not hungry, and I want to go back to sleep and not wake up until summer at home. Dad helped me eat jello and an applesauce, he ate the sandwich and joked that he's had better cardboard, I managed a smile but it hurt.

I asked what all was wrong with me. Dad started to explain what the doctors had told him but it started my head spinning more for a few minutes. Dad said Sara was in a coma, a medical one because she was hurt so badly. My poor sister, does she know her best friend died? She was right there, right next to Katie in the helicopter when she passed away. My legs started to throb and my right arm was covered in white bandages.

"Am I going to be ok?" I asked. Dad said they'll have to put me in physical therapy for my legs, I broke both of the big bones and my right arm was badly broken also. Sara had a tube in her chest because a rib broke and poked a hole in her lung. Dad said Sara had brain swelling and many broken bones also. I had these big metal rods with little rods fastened to them going into my legs. My right knee was dangling from metal work attached around my bed holding my leg in the air. Dad said my right knee was broken and there were metal wires in to hold it together.

That day doctors came in, the Josh Hartnett looking guy was cute but in blue gray scrubs that didn't look good on him, his partner was a very cute light skinned girl, her hair was in a ponytail and her makeup looked fresh, it must be the beginning of their day. They poked my toes with their pens and asked me to count the pokes. They told me the rods will hold my bones together until they heal then rehab will help me to strengthen my muscles. The intern resident people didn't stay long but they said they'll have to change the bandages tomorrow and they'll see me again then.

I started crying again, I miss Sara, Katie and mommy. My legs hurt, throb and itch. My arm itches, all of these bandages itch and I can't scratch them. This is awful and I can't stop crying. Dad looks so helpless and so very scared. Dad said Mr. Matt stayed in the hospital for half the day before going home to Tell Ryann the news about his sister. Dad felt so bad that Mr. Matt lost his daughter and that there was a part of dad that lost the same daughter.

I'm tired again. I feel so groggy and want to be outside. Dad opened the shades a bit to let in sunlight to help take my mind off being stuck in this hospital. Nurses come and go checking my monitors that beep and put that arm thing on me and take my temperature. Dad flicks the eight hospital channels and gripes before settling on the same talk show junk each time. Dad said tomorrow after they change my wrappings that he'll go trade places with mom.

I told him he needs to go to her hospital and have coffee with mom before letting her come here. He said I shouldn't worry about them and that they're big kids, then he actually smiled a bit. I begged him to please to have a coffee with her, I worry about them, two daughters in hospitals and who knows what's ahead. I wonder how Sara is doing. I can't get comfortable with my leg hanging in the air and my butt is sore from lying here all day.

My anxiety is creeping up, I want to go walk around, I want to be free of this metal contraption, and I want my comfy bed and the quiet without all of this beeping. Dad found a news channel that reviewed yet another Detroit loss. I hear him sigh but at least it's getting his mind off things. I asked him about Sara, he said no changes. Docs say she'll be in the coma for a few days and in the I.C.U for a week after that. Sara had a brain bleed and a lot of injuries. I want to be with Sara, and I wish Katie was alive and ok.

Dad said I should rest, how am I supposed to relax when I've been lying here all day? I haven't done anything. The sun is starting to set and the sky was dark gray, looks like it's going to snow. I can see the house tops across the parking lot, there are spots of snow on some of them, they'll look more pretty covered completely in snow. I wish Katie was alive.

Dad said he got a text from mom, the truck that hit us had 3 people in it, they all were ok just some bumps and bruises and that's all the police told her. Dad went to the cafeteria for coffee; he said he'd pick up some munchies for me. The nurse brought a dinner tray while he was gone, she also put some medication into the tube that went into my arm and asked how I was doing. She was nice but seemed too rushed to chat then ran off again.

Another brown tray with a brown lid covering a plate of something with a side of jello on it sits on the table cart by my bed, "oh scrumptious" I thought sarcastically. This time it's green jello instead of red, I'm not hungry. The drone of the TV almost drowns out the commotion of the hallway; it's full of nurses and people calling out on their paging things. Dad came back in, it took him a long time, I'm sure he needed to stretch being cooped up in this room all night and day.

Dad said he ran into some people at the coffee machine, he said that two of them were in the truck and that they were staying with the driver. He said they felt terrible about everything that happened and sent many apologies. It was a husband and wife and her brother, the driver was the husband and that the airbag fractured his sternum. They had said the back end of the truck just swung out and then they hit our car. The wife started crying upon hearing that Katie lost her life and gave my dad their number to text if a fund was established in her name or if they could help in anyway.

I thought it was very nice of them to offer but it wasn't going to bring her back. I was mad, and sad, and angry and I started crying again. Dad held me for a while and we both cried. I wish I was home, I wish Sara and I were both at home, sprawled out on the couch watching some rom com and giggling at how cheesy it was. I wish all of us girls were lounging around laughing together, Sara and Katie, Bobbi and I while mom laughed at us. Dad said mom wished she was with me.

Dad said he would convince mom to have coffee with him, he said she was being stubborn and that her girls needed someone with them, he said I was being adamant about it and that both of us girls were going to be ok for a bit. Dad hit my nurse button and the afternoon lady came in. Dad asked if there was something available to help me sleep. I didn't want to take anything but I was so tired, my body was drained but my anxiety wasn't going to let me sleep. She brought me an oval white pill and an itty bitty swallow of water.

I took the pill but went back to crying. Dad tried to talk to me to calm me down but I was crying too hard to hear more than a mutter. Dad calmed me down and convinced me to eat. I got down the jello and fruit cup. I got half way through the apple before starting to feel sick so dad ate the cardboard sandwich for me. It was dark out now and I could see the little white and silver glistening specks of snow falling in the street light reflections. The noise in the hallway was a dull rumble mixed with the beeps of machines and the occasional squeaky wheel of something rolling by.

My head was heavy and my pillow soaked with tears. I could feel my hair sticking to my head and to my ears. My left ear was full of tears and it made everything sound like an underwater muffle. I didn't want to fall asleep in this place again, my lower back hurt from lying in one position so long, my legs hurt from not moving them, everything itched from these bandages. I feel like a mummy but am partially covered in this light blue gown with dark blue circular patterns on it.

Dad put two more blankets on me; they were also plain hospital white just like everything else around me. The wood floor grew darker and the shadows on the corners of the walls got bigger. I don't want to sleep, I want to be better and be free of this cage. The bars of this cell aren't on the doors but a half halo that I am locked to. Dad pulled his chair around and kicked his feet up on my left side.

I stared out the window at the falling snow, the flakes were light but each speckle was calming. The reflection on the window of the nurses' station showed ladies and a few gentlemen moving around. A nurse came in with the arm squeeze thing and took my temperature again. She looked at the beeping monitor then asked me if I needed anything. She suggested I try and rest and told me she'll be back in a few hours.

My eyes won't stay open but the tears are still leaking from them. My cheeks are cold from being wet. Dad was trying to get comfortable cause I could hear him wrestling into a cozy position for the night. Dad started telling me that they may move me into another room since this one was just the post-op ward. Dad said he'll wait till they move me before trading places with mom, err joining her for coffee then swapping.

I can't get comfortable with my right arm propped up on these pillows and the noise. I'm so tired, my head is pulsing and my headache is coming back. I can't keep fighting this throbbing headache nor want to. I try to open my eyes but they are so watery that all I see is a blur. I want to watch the snowflakes fall. I want to get up and walk to the car where dad is waiting. I can feel some of the warmth from dads' feet at my side.

I love my dad so much, it has to be so uncomfortable for him to have to sit in that chair and try to sleep. I wonder how Ryann took the news of Katie. I wonder how Mr. Matt was handling Katie's death. Did Sara know Katie was dying while lying next to her? Was Sara awake or aware of what was going on when she was trapped in the car? Could Sara hear me screaming?

I feel my body go limp; I can no longer feel the dull throbbing of my lower body. The itches that bothered me all day have gone away. My eyes are still leaking and feeling heavier. I can feel the tightness in my chest lift and my heart-beat slow down. The noise in the hallway is becoming quiet, suddenly the glass screams from the accidents crackle and screech like a banshee through my mind. My shoulders lurch forward a bit before I relax as the darkness sets in and the weight of my blankets ease.

chapter 6

THE MORNING STARTED abruptly, there was a big nurse guy at my side with the arm squeezy thing going "phff phff phff" as it squeezed harder and harder. Dad was still in his claimed spot right by my side. The nurse guy asked how I was feeling and all I could come up with was an unspeakable sound that sounded like a baby deer.

The nurse said he'll look into another round of pain meds for me then he left. Dad said I need to do better at eating breakfast today. He helped me eat the pancakes but the orange juice burned my throat. The tube hanging out of me hurts, my downstairs hurts, my butt hurts, my legs are sore from not moving. The nurse came back with a peach colored pill and another itty bitty gulp of water.

Dad said I tossed and turned all night. He said he's sure my right leg is hurting from tugging at the metal pin work that is sticking out of me. The two doctors from yesterday came in with a cart covered in bandages and tape. The kinda cute guy looks like he hadn't slept since I saw him last and she was still bright eyed but slouched a bit more today. They told me that changing the bandages might be a shock, things will hurt a bit but seeing the mess of my legs might be a scary sight.

They un-wrapped my left leg slowly, cutting most of the band aids off, bits of it stuck to blood that dried on my skin. God my leg looks awful; it's green and purple with bruises all over my thigh. Oh how embarrassing, my parts are just open to the cute doc and it looks terrible with that hose sticking out of it. It hurts and things "down there" look so rough and uncomfortable.

Dad kept his back turned as the doctors worked, he couldn't bear to see his baby girl hurting. The doctors used baby wipes to clean my skin and showed me the two holes that stuck into my thigh muscle that screwed into the bone on one end then to the rod that ran along my leg. They then started on the right leg.

It took longer for the doctors to attend to my right leg; they had to work around the bar going through my knee. They warned me to brace myself because it was about to get ugly. The girl doc tossed a washcloth on my lady bits to keep them covered as they worked, I appreciated the dignity. They began unwrapping, starting and the mid shin and even that far down looked dark from what I could see. I had a hard time seeing past my knee and the wires holding it together. I could feel the pain and pressure against my knee with each gentle tug of the wraps.

They un-wrapped my knee and it was hideous. My knee was big and swollen and there was a piece of white tape running down over my knee cap and under it I could see the skin pinched together with staples running under the tape, my skin looked tight and red. My knee is deep green and very purple. As they uncovered my right thigh the colors got darker and there was ooze around the one lower hole in my leg. The doctors used a brush to clean around the hole with a brown substance that ran down and onto the sheets.

My right thigh was so dark and looked bumpy, the muscles twitched as they cut away the wrappings and the leg swung in the wires a bit that had me tied in. The lady doctor washed my leg with a wipe and they started re-wrapping me. My legs looked so horrible. How bad will the scars be? The small holes will probably disappear but the scar on my knee looks like a Frankenstein like monster leg.

I'm tired from the jostling. Dad said he's going to make the long drive to see Sara and mom. He's stretching and trying to work out a kink in his back but he's trying to look tough for me. Dad asked if I needed anything and that I was sure I was ok with him leaving. I told him I was still super sad about Katie. He said he was too. Dad gave me a big hug and told me how much he loved me and was very grateful that I was still here and going to be ok. We hugged as the nurse came in to tell us that I was going to be moved to the seventh floor which is the rehab floor.

Dad asked if I wanted him to stay until I was comfortable in my new real estate. I told dad to go and spend an hour with mom and to let the family know things were ok. I asked him to ask mom to grab my laptop from home and my comfy fleece robe. I missed my pink flannel fleece robe. Dad was texting mom about my wishes and told her he would make the stop if she wasn't up for it. Nurses and transporters showed up to escort me to my new digs and dad headed out for the time being.

The move was awkward, I don't think I like being paraded through the hospital with people looking at my leg suspended in the air and a hose with a bag on the end hanging from my privates. The bumps in and out of the elevator were rough. I hope dads drive went more smoothly than mine did. I wonder if he was scared to see Sara, in a coma, full of tubes and unresponsive. I'm lucky that I'll be ok but I'm still scared. My heart aches for the Matts, I wish Katie was here making jokes and whistling at the hot doctors and making dj noises with the monitor beeping to make us laugh.

My new room had pale green walls but a bright white window facing more tree tops. I'm sure the move only took a few minutes but I wish mom was here already. I wonder if I can go to Sara's hospital and that we could share a room like we did when we were little girls. We had our own rooms but I kept sneaking in to her room so much when I was three that mom and dad bought her bunk beds, for us. Those bunk beds eventually came in handy for sleepovers but I loved having the bottom bunk with my big sis sleeping just above me.

I wonder if Sara also has a tube in her downstairs like I do. Why am I thinking about her downstairs? Dad said she had a tube in her chest, what does that mean? How am I tired, again? I haven't done anything nor gone anywhere, more or less. My eyes started watering with a yawn and that's all it took to start me crying about Katie again. Was she scared or hurting? Did she just fall asleep and never wake up? Was she dreaming of happy things when she passed on, or were the glass screams of the accident bellowing in her mind the last thoughts she'd had? I feel so bad, how am I going to deal with the hurt in my heart for her and the glad I have that Sara and I are alive?

My butt hurts and I can't get comfortable. The tube in me feels like its sticking to my leg and is pulling at the tape that has it tethered to my thigh. How do boys deal with their parts where they are? How do they just have things there all the time, the discomfort must be rough. I've seen boy parts in books and stuff on anatomy and sure during sex-ed in school all of us girls peeked and made small cracks but tried not to laugh out loud so we didn't get in trouble. Why am I thinking about boy private parts?

This all in one remote thing is as simple as it can be but it sucks because if you drop the bloody thing you can't page a nurse to help you pick it up. There needs to be more than eight channels, three of them are super boring and one is just about the hospital, blah blah blah tons of employees, blah blah lots of floors. The other channels are boring news stuff and idiots fighting about who knows what in some junky country full of nut jobs that only fight and kill themselves instead of fighting to educate themselves or getting clean water to drink.

I miss my home, I miss being home. How long am I going to be here? It might be getting close to lunch time. I hope mom is coming soon. The tree tops across the parking lot in my window are swaying a bit more than earlier when I first got here, I wonder if it's cold out. Friday was cold but Sara had the car warm when she picked me up from school. We dropped Katie off at home to get ready for the concert and get homework done. We were all so giddy about the concert and couldn't wait to go.

I can't believe I'll never see Katie again, she was smiling and cheerful Friday, not even two whole days ago and now she's gone. No more playing at the park, no more Katie. How is Sara going to take the bad news? She is going to feel terrible that she was driving. I know she is going to blame herself and have nightmares. How are we going get through all of this and get on with our lives? I keep staring at the trees and think back to days at the park playing with Katie.

How is Sara going to handle everything? Is she going to make it through her coma stuff? Watching the tree tops sway back and forth, they start to blur into a white light as my eyes begin to water again. Once again I'm crying and now there isn't anyone around to hold me. How is mom dealing with Katie's passing on? I know mom loved having Katie as a third daughter. I remember one time Sara and Katie were laughing so hard milk spurt out of Katie's nose and all mom could do was look at her with a very quizzical look and say "I'm glad YOU didn't slide out of me" which then caused milk to rocket out of Sara's nose too.

When is my mom going to be here? This tube in my privates is rubbing and things feel so very chafed and irritated. The tape on my leg hurts and it pulls. I can't get into a position that takes the pressure off of my tailbone. The beeping of the monitor above me is getting annoying and I don't want to be here anymore. I wonder what Bobbi is doing and if she knows what happened. What happened to my phone? Dad said the officer answered my phone but does that mean it ended up at a police station or what?

When am I going back to school? How long will I have to be stuck in bed? Why am I so tired from not doing anything? My legs hurt, my arm throbs and I can't itch any of it. A new nurse came in to do the squeezy arm thing and check my signs again. This nurse was another guy; he had patchy facial hair and a haircut that made him look like toadstool from the Mario brother games. This nurse was quiet and was quick with his work and asked if my pain was manageable. I told him I was hurting again so he said he'd have to check my record to see when I was due to more meds. My right arm wasn't changed when my legs were and the nurse told me that the wraps on my arm may need to be changed soon.

The nurse was off to another patient's room but reassured me that he'd be back. I cried myself to sleep again. Minutes into an awful uncomfortable nap the glass screams intruded into my head and I lurched awake. The pain in my legs surged through me like I was in the car accident all over again. My shoulders lurched forward and my heart is racing again. My head is starting to pound and it feels like the backs of my eyes are being kicked at again. My eyes are watering with tears again. I'm tired of hurting.

The nurse came in again and with pain meds. I took my dose and I'm really glad his timing was on. It seemed to take twenty minutes for the meds to work and I cried until they did. I miss Sara, and Katie, I want my mom to hurry up. I hope mom and dad enjoy their coffee time but I want one of them here with me. My eyelids started closing through the tears and even though I fought them, they still closed anyways. The pain subsided for a bit and I was able to go back to sleep again.

"Sweetie" I fought to open my eyes as the blur cleared, mom was standing over me; I started to cry again finally seeing her. Mom hugged me so tightly and even though I could feel the pull of my legs and arm I didn't care, I held her back with my good arm as we both cried. We both tried to sniffle to clear the runny noses and after a few hard sniffs we were almost in sync. We kind of chuckled between the weeping but it didn't quell the tears of joy we had holding each other.

I asked how Sara was doing. Mom said Sara was in rough shape and it's going to be a rough road to get her back to normal. Sara had the left side of her head shaved because they had to drill a hole in the side of her head to relieve pressure and they won't know for a while if there will be any permanent damage but things went well. Sara also had a feeding tube, breathing tube and a tube jammed into her ribs to remove fluid that was collapsing her lung.

Mom continued to describe that because Sara was pinned against the steering wheel it kept her from being crushed from the sides but that it broke some ribs, her left arm was casted and her face was really bruised. I started crying again thinking about my poor sister. Do people dream in comas? Mom said the doctors are keeping her in the coma for a week or so to keep her activity down and help her heal better. Mom said she felt awful for Mr. Matt and is deeply saddened for the loss of Katie also.

My nurse guy Mark brought in my dinner tray, I still have no appetite. Mom sat in Dads chair and just held my hand for a while. Mom looks like she's been mugged in a rainstorm, she needs rest but I was so glad she was by my side. Mom helped me to eat dinner, I really didn't eat then either, I managed down another Jell-O and applesauce and half of the mashed potatoes but my throat still hurt so badly. Mark brought my afternoon pain meds and a few extra blankets. It was getting dark out and even though I was exhausted I didn't want to sleep.

Mom and I talked about Katie. We told stories of her being goofy and how terribly we were going to miss her. She was so vibrant and full of life, neither of us could believe how bad we already missed her. We both stayed weepy and tried to fight it with small laughs but neither of us could laugh or smirk off the pure hurt we felt at the loss of our friend. Mom said Mr. Matt was heartbroken. Mr. Matt was going to have to try to plan a funeral and dad was going to help out a lot.

Mom thanked me for encouraging her and dad to spend an hour having coffee. Dad was going to try to work this week since Sara was safe in a hospital bed and the nurses watching her had both cell phone numbers and dad was also going to help Mr. Matt as much as he could. Neither of my parents could imagine losing a child, both were so very close and that started moms crying which then began my tears again. My eyes feel so puffy from crying.

Mom said she and dad spoke about how they were going to handle having two kids in two different hospitals; mom was going to stay with me full time or mostly for the next week and take things from there. They said they were going to look into maybe moving me to Sara's hospital so they could better be in both places since home was in the middle and the drive sucked. Mom had a bag with her that she had quickly filled on the brief stop at home. Mom brought my laptop and I was glad to see it as it could get me online and watch movies instead of the judge shows and gossip nonsense that plagued the TV.

My eyes were heavy and my head started to pound again. I don't want to fall asleep, I have my mom and I don't want her to disappear in the night. I feel my head getting weak and starting to sink into the pillow again. The sky grows dark and mom turns down the lights in my room to match. Mom sets the chair next to me like dad had and takes her position next to her youngest daughter. Mom snuggles up under the blankets Mark brought and asks if I need anything. I was complacent that she was by my side but I was still so severely uncomfortable. My legs had a dull throb to them and my right shoulder was starting to hurt from the lack of movement.

Crack the screams of shattering glass pierced the quiet that had almost set in as I closed my eyes and was readying myself for slumber. I lunged forward, my body uncontrollably reacted. I gasped for breath. Mom jumped almost as much as I did. Dad warned her that I didn't sleep soundly but I startled her none the less. Mom asked if she could do anything and tried to comfort me, it took me a second to regain my awareness and realize I was in the hospital and not trapped in the car anymore being nauseated with burning chemical smells and the flashing lights.

Mom stroked my hair and ran her fingers through it until I fell asleep. The next morning she was curled up in the same chair dad was the morning before. I awoke to the pains in my body and all over. Mark was here again and bid me a good morning as he took my blood pressure. He warned me that I was on the list for bandage changes for my right arm and the residents were making rounds. Mom woke up and took a minute to gain her composure; she washed her face and made her way to get some coffee. A pretty girl came in dressed in operating scrubs, the same bluish gray that the other two doctors' people were wearing when my leg wraps were changed.

Mom didn't shy away like dad did when they changed my leg bandages. My right arm was also very green and purple and in some areas it looked black. My arm was the size of my leg before the accident, it was huge swollen and it hurt to even try to make my fingers move. I had a large cut with gross black stitches on the under part of my arm and they told me they had to put some kind of plate to hold the bone pieces together.

The pretty lady doc, whom kinda looked like a tan Claire Forlani with a pretty smile, warned me that it will take some time for my arm to heal. She also spoke to mom that my upper arm was also broken and they will cast it once the forearm heals better. The doctor lady, Mika, was very gentle and wrapped gauze between my fingers then poked each fingertip asking me to identify how may pokes I felt and to which finger. She could tell I was becoming more uncomfortable and the pain was getting worse from the workout. She reassured my mom I was due for some meds but that I should eat more before then.

Mark came in and had to empty the bag hanging out of me. I was so embarrassed but he also had to look between my legs to make sure things were as they should be. I was so ashamed and I couldn't even look at him, I had toad from Mario brothers looking at my intimate parts. Oh god mom is making comments about how irritated I am down there, I want to die. He said mild irritation was common as having a catheter was abnormal for a body and its location. I stared out the window as hard as I could; hoping maybe I'd zap out there and not be here.

Mom helped Mark cover me up and thanked him for his help, as he exited he let us know the breakfast cart was just down the hall. I looked at mom and she must have seen the horror on my face, she said she was sorry I had to go through that. I started to weep again. I told her I have had a pain down there since before the tube was rammed into my delicate area and it's been hurting for days now. I couldn't tell dad and I can't tell a stranger around here, that's a very personal issue. Mom asked me about "the pain", was it a pressure, cramp like, similar to a rash, or an infection? I began to tell her is felt like a sharp pain before we were interrupted for breakfast.

chapter 7

MOM AND I spoke for a bit as she helped me to eat breakfast. I still had a measly appetite but she warned me that continuing to take the pain meds might make me sick if I don't keep up on eating. I explained that my down there pain had sharp shooting pains in addition to all of my other pains, she wondered if maybe because so much of me hurt "things" just decided to join in. She then reminded me that boy privates think on their own, not ours hahaha.

Mom asked me what happened the night of the concert. I knew she wanted to know but also didn't want to have to ask me to relive it. I relived enough of the crunching shrieking metal sounds and hard thuds and glass screams enough already. The banshee like howls of the shattering glass haunted my sleep. I can hear the glass exploding and the car imploding whenever I close my eyes. I began to recreate the concert for mom, Darius rocking to family tradition, Lady A covering every great song they have, the lead singer jiggling on the piano, the guitarist playing more instruments than the rest of the band combined, men dancing with their ladies, Sara, Katie and myself shouting and singing along to every word that we knew.

I described the cow corralling and how we felt like sheep all boxed in trying to snake our way to the exit. I laughed about the cowboys dancing in the back of their trucks shaking their hind ends and Katie hooting and hollering at them, mom laughed a little with tears in her eyes. I spoke about us being "east bound and down" and heading home, laughing and goofing off recapping the awesome show we had all shared, now the only we'd ever share with Katie again.

I described the flash of light from the truck next to us and how quickly it all happened, but in slow motion, I told her that dad ran into the two passengers of the truck and she acknowledged he told her. I told her about how I was trapped, my arm in shearing pain and my legs pinned and how nothing moved, the seatbelt squeezing me and keeping me from being able to scream, the burning smell that kept choking me and burning my eyes, nose and lungs. Tears began to stream down moms face and she looked at me with a sense of helplessness and longing to have been there for me.

I told her about the screams and gargling sound of life leaving Katie and moans of Sara as we were all trapped in that wreck. I then began to tell mom that I dazed in and out and don't remember a whole lot but then waking up in the ambulance, the wailing cries of the siren and crappy noise from the radio. I told her about Walker talking to me and the visions of tubes and a cellphone I could make out from under the cloth on my face. Moms head lifted and her crying ceased for a moment, "cellphone?" she asked. I replied that I had seen a scratched orange blackberry a few times after the tears had cleared my eyes and before the next welling up of my eyes.

"He shouldn't have been on a cellphone baby" mom expressed, her sadness became concern rather quickly. I told her I wasn't sure what was going on and that I kept closing my eyes and that my head kept spinning. I remember my head feeling wet and that my hair was sticking to everything laying there. Mom grabbed my head and turned it in each direction with intent. Mom said I only had bruising on my head and no cut or bleeding so I shouldn't have needed bandaging on my face. I was getting scared at mom's reactions to my accident.

Mom turned from scared to concerned, she asked me to continue telling her about the ambulance ride. I described feeling the cold on my legs, the things swinging in and out of the crack in my vision. I described the terrible metal music on the radio and the driver shouting into a radio. I recall some of the radio sounds like "eta" and "the hospital is awaiting your arrival" things like that. Mom kept me talking.

Lunch came and went as did Mark, my day nurse guy. As the sky grew dark I kept explaining everything I remembered from the night, from the accident to the emergency room, being skewered with this hose in my little lady down below to the scan thing that left a nasty taste in my mouth. Mom asked Mark about my personal belongings I arrived in. He brought her a clear bag with blue writing on it. Wow the bag had a lot of bloody stuff in it.

Mark brought my afternoon meds right after the dinner tray arrived. My legs began to hurt again and my anxiety came and went as mom and I spoke. Mom laid out my clothes on the floor. I wasn't sure I wanted to see my purple flannel shirt all ripped up and blood stained, my blue jean skirt cut up the side and my pink undies in tatters. Seeing the clothes as mom held them up flashed memories of the wreck into my head. Every time mom held up an article of my ensemble, glass fell to the floor and the sound of the glass made me shutter.

Mom held up my cute little boots and the suede was blood stained and glass poured out of them when mom turned them over. Mom then picked up the undershirt I wear because I don't feel big enough for a bra yet; it was also cut up the front and stained in blood. It looked like I had been shot and stabbed while wearing it. The lace that lined the top of the shirt was still covered in vomit and mom carefully held it up to not touch any of it.

Mom said she didn't see my white leggings that she recalled me wearing before I left. Where are they? I was wearing them under my skirt because it's cold in February and they were so cute with my skirt, plus I'm very conservative and don't want my body being flaunted all over the place. Even my socks were soaked in blood and still damp. Mom had to wash her hands after handling my clothes and then she swept up the glass that had sprinkled all over the floor.

I kept talking to mom but could feel myself dizzying and growing tired again. The numb throbbing of my legs and arm started to get harder, mom could tell I was fighting to stay awake. The noise from out at the nurse' station was constant but came into my right ear; it seemed to make my head spin more. I could feel tears begin to run down my cheeks again and mom sat there with me as I cried myself to sleep. Mom sat at my side and stroked my hair until I don't remember anymore, I felt safe and relieved she was here.

I woke up early to the light from behind the blinds and Mark once again welcoming me to the day as he place the blood thing on my arm. He said they were working on making rounds and that I was due for a surgical evaluation again, meaning a big day of changing Band-Aids again. He smiled a bit at his own joke but caught on quick I was too tired and that it was too early for jokes.

Mom came into my room right before the breakfast tray. Mom said she had been working on a few things while I slept. Mom said she asked for a hospital counselor for me to talk with about the accident to help me cope and also had spent an hour dealing with the emergency admitting people to make sure there wasn't anything left out of my belongings bag. Mom was up to something, I just knew it. I don't remember dreaming much, I don't remember being haunted with the sounds of the accident last night, mom said she asked them to give me something to help me sleep better, I was still tired and felt groggy but it must have worked.

"Mom, please tell me what's on your mind" I asked her bluntly. She replied that she was just curious about a few things. She texted my dad that I was awake and he said "hi" to me. He was at work but only half the day. Today is the first of two days that were to be Katie's memorial then funeral. I can't believe they are going to bury her. I missed her so much and I started crying again. Mark came in to warn me that the Docs were on their way.

Mark left quickly as he saw mom and I needing a moment and we could hear him ask the residents to hold off a few minutes. It was kind of Mark to notice and I guess a lot of nurses are akin to moments like this. Mika and the kinda cute other resident came in; it was time to check my legs again. They asked how I was feeling and how my pain has been, I told them it's been awful and mom piped up and mentioned a lot of discomfort.

The doctors got me unwrapped and then rewrapped and mom was watching what they were doing the whole time. Mom asked how long until the staples that were holding my knee in were going to come out and how long until my knee was going to be freed from the bear trap looking thing that has my right knee as its prisoner. My legs are still purple and dark green and big and ugly. My muscles are so sore and I just want to be off my hurting butt and walk around.

Mom looked over my legs and helped the doctors clean me up before they repackaged me. I could tell mom had something on her mind; she was antsy and was trying to hurry the doctors along. The doctors said once I was out of the leg swing they wanted to get an MRI so see my legs and the tendons and things. There wasn't a thing I could do but nod and wince as they wound the wraps around me. Mom was asking questions like what all did they do in the operating room and how long until the swelling goes down. The doctors were very vague and only answered with "she'll progress in time but it all takes time". Way to duck an answer.

Once the surgeons were gone and off to another patients room mom was back to her prodding me with questions. She asked me more about the ambulance ride; she wasn't as curios about the accident. Mom had me lay back and close my eyes and retrace each moment that I remembered. I remembered lying on the stretcher and feeling the glass stab into my head, the wrap around my eyes and the cold on my legs. I remember feeling the straps squeeze into my stomach and my chest.

Mom asked me why my legs felt cold and not more than the rest of me. I told her I only felt the sheet on my skin and my wet hair sticking to me. I felt dizzy and sick as the ambulance bumped and turned. I can feel the tears filling my eyes again. I remember being so scared lying there and not knowing what was going on around me and also wondering what happened to Sara and Katie. Mom reassured me that she was here and that I was safe and that everything was ok.

I remember trying to open my eyes to look around between bouts of feeling ill, Walker kept telling me to relax and lay back and that we were in route to the hospital. I kept asking him about Sara and Katie but he didn't know anything about them. The sirens' wailing kept echoing in chorus with the sounds of the accident that seem to be imprinted in my brain. Mom was texting dad and nodding along with what I had to say. I asked her what was going on; she just said he was curious to know what was going on.

I kept opening my eyes when I was recalling what was going on because I kept getting scared and I wanted to see my mom. Mom reassured me to keep talking. I remember seeing the cell phone swoop in and out of my view with the bumps of the ambulance and he must have been texting or something. I remember seeing bags and clear tubes shaking with my body as we bumped our way to the hospital. I told her Walker kept saying that I'd be ok and to just relax. Mom asked what else I felt and what else happened. I told her I just felt cold and pain all over.

Mom texted dad some more and then the dinner tray came in. I ate a bit then mom ducked into the bathroom for a shower. I opened my laptop to scroll through pictures I had, ones of Katie in her plays or Sara and I as little girls. I started to cry again looking through the pictures and each one made me happy with memories and then sad that these are all the pictures I'll ever have of us. Mom finished her shower and came out to join me in looking at the pictures.

We finished the night tearing up and joking a bit about Katie. The night set in and the lights faded out, the murmur of the hallway didn't break a dull roar but it didn't take long for my new night nurse to bring me sleeping meds and then it was time to sleep again. I remember mom stroking my hair and shushing me to sleep. Visions of the accident played in my mind; I kept seeing the flash of lights veer into Katie's door. I remember wondering if she knew what happened. How long was she scared or in pain before passing away? Did she pass on with the thoughts of the concert in her head or memories of her childhood?

I jumped awake in the night thinking that in mere hours Katie would be promised to the ground forever. To visit her ever again will be at a headstone in a marble park. I woke up with tears in my eyes and as I woke up, it was dark but I could feel the tears multiply. The sounds of people talking in the hall way blended with the sounds of people hurrying in the background during the accident, I can't tell them apart.

I wasn't awake for long before crying myself to sleep again. Was Sara dreaming? How was Sara going to feel when she woke up to find out that Katie died and was buried and that neither of us could have attended the funeral. I woke back up in the morning and called for mom. Mom answered my call and I desperately needed her to go to Katie's funeral service. I couldn't be there and neither could Sara, mom and dad have to go.

Mom understood and was texting with dad. They agreed to meet at home then offered to pick up Mr. Matt and Ryann. The Matts had Mr. Matts' mom drive them when they went to the church for the service. I laid in my bed, my butt was sore and legs burned and itched while I just wondered what the service was like. Was the service like I had seen on TV? Was everyone crying and wondering why her? Did half the school show up? All of the students that were in varsity blues with her, coaches and teachers? I wonder how many students were able to go.

It's Tuesday now and I'm growing weary of laying here. Mark came and went and kept track of my blood pressure and vital signs. He didn't talk much but always asked if there was anything I needed. I felt kinda bad but the Mario Brothers tune kept playing in my mind as he moved along. I wanted to whistle it as he left the room and for a moment as I had a vision of him getting hit by a turtle shell then spinning out and hitting the nurse' station, I smiled a bit. Katie would have made the funny video game noises.

I lay there all morning and couldn't even look at the lunch tray. Mark changed my IV bag but didn't say anything about the untouched lunch. I watched the tree tops sway in the window and wondered if maybe Katie was shaking them to let me know she was still here. I watched the trees sway back and forth, I pictured back to a day at the park, Katie, Sara and I walking around and wandering to the giant rock we painted on occasion to support Sara's cross country team. I loved just sitting at a picnic table listening to Sara and Katie talk about school, Varsity Blues, running, homework and teachers.

Katie wanted to act in college, she wanted to become a social worker and help kids. Katie was so alive and loved life, now she's lying in a casket surrounded by people crying and missing her, like I'm lying here in a hospital bed. My eyes are sore and puffy from all the crying but I can't stop it. I miss my mom, dad and sister but dad and mom need to be with the Matt's right now and Sara is trapped at a different hospital, kept from me.

I couldn't imagine how Mr. Matt is feeling. How hard would it be to have to bury your child? It kills me to think of burying my mom or dad but I also know it goes against nature for a parent to have to bury their children. In the end we as children are all supposed to outlive our parents, I can't believe I was so close to dying. One small patch of ice claimed one young girls' life and barely spared two others'.

Will Ryann become more of a shut in? Will he get over having to become an only child without Katie as a buffer between him and his father? I have so many thoughts running through my head. The trees slow in their dancing. The sun seems to brighten up a bit as the clouds part. Is it warm enough that everyone that follows the hearse to the cemetery won't freeze?

Will there be a giant funeral precession that winds and crawls along the cemetery pathways? Will the lowering of the casket make those that cry, cry harder? Will it be like so many funerals I've seen on TV? Everyone dressed in black, singing Amazing Grace and through the tears, the head funeral director will slowly lower the casket, a long slow last time Mr. Matt will ever see his only daughter.

I can't see the trees now; everything is a blur of tears as my eyes once again welled up. How long after someone passes away is it until they are forgotten? Will people look back in a year with a quick memory? Will they call her name out during Graduation? I vow to name my first daughter after my other sister, Katie Matt. Will the pastor whom sounds like Donald Sutherland; say a psalm about healing or about mourning?

Will there be a passage about the cycle of life, beginnings and ends? Are mom and dad feeling guilty that both of their daughters lived and Katie didn't? Are they sitting in the back of the church ducking away or near the front to help comfort Mr. Matt? Do people know that Sara and I are in the hospital or will they just think we couldn't make it? How old will I be when I pass away? Will it be like that scary movie where death will come for me because it let me slip through its fingers? Will Sara pass away in the hospital?

My anxiety is acting up, my heart rate is rising and mom isn't here. I want to be at the funeral, I want Katie to know how much she meant to me. I want my other sister back. The tears are streaming down my left side, the pillow is wet and the tears coming from my right eye make my noise itch as they cross and join the tears from my left eye on my pillow. Mark came in with more meds, he says that I should rest and try not to get too worked up; he can see that my heart rate is going fast on my noisy monitor.

I have movies saved onto my laptop but I just want the quiet. The screams of the accident still echo in my head when I close my eyes. Just laying here is maddening; I wish I could be at the funeral. I wish I could tell

Katie how much she truly meant, I wish this never happened. I wish Michigan didn't have all these budget issues so they could have salted better or something.

I just laid there staring out the window for half the day, watching the tree tops sway gently or not at all. The sky was cloudy but you could tell the sun was behind them, warm, encouraging, supportive, just like Katie was for me. Katie's smile was bright and a life giving source and she always brightened someone's day. I never thought any of this could ever have happened. I miss Sara, mom and dad so much. I miss being at home and lounging around the house, I even miss being at school right now. I miss my life.

I wonder how Bobbi is doing. I wonder if she'll visit soon. I wonder how many people know what happened. I'm sure mom or dad spoke with Principal Marl and got my assignments and such from her. I don't want to do my homework but I know if things wait too long I'll have a ton of it. My legs are hurting again and my right hand tingles and it's starting to throb. I feel gross and I want a shower. How long until my legs return to a normal size? I feel fat and lumpy like that pig looking Kim girl from TV, it's disgusting.

My eyes keep watering and I'm tired of crying. I think half of the fluids that slowly drip into my arm are leaking out of my face. I'm tired of the running nose, the sore eyes from crying and the pain. My whole body hurts and I'm sore all over. My tail bone hurts from half laying in this position, I can't even move my bed because I'm wired into this contraption and I can't do anything about it.

Why did all of this have to happen? Why did Katie have to die? I'm sick of this hospital food but I have no appetite anyways. I can still feel glass embedded into me and the small sharp pains just blend into the rest of the pains I feel. My feet are cold and feel swollen but they hurt to try to wiggle. The doctors told me to be as still as possible and just let my injuries heal but I have to move, I want to run, jump and play. I wish I wasn't trapped laying here, I'm losing my mind.

Eighth grade was almost over, I get that getting though school was the biggest part to school, mere survival, I thought that was hard enough. When will I get back to school, will I be on crutches or spend the rest of my life limping? Will I be pretty and dance again? Will Bobbi and I get to go to spring school dances and make fun of fellow classmates for being all nervous but in their hurry to kiss one another? Eighth grade seemed so lame, that limbo between being a child and growing into your real teen years. The social oddities of missing playing jump rope as a little girl and acting much more grown up and taking a liking to what all the older girls liked.

I'm so alone. Mark hung out with me for a few minutes but had to return to his rounds. I don't know Mark but I appreciate that he tried to comfort me a bit. I didn't even turn to watch him leave with subtle hopes that he'd be hit by a cartoon turtle shell or slip on a big banana peel and spin out. I'm getting tired again and my chest is hurting. I can't breathe and I'm getting light headed again.

I'm going to really miss Katie so much, I already do. Katie would stick up for me if Sara got annoyed with me. Katie mocked Sara when Sara was cranky and it never took long for Sara to be laughing at Katie. Katie could make anyone laugh, and she did. Katie had great grades and never seemed to have to try; everything she did seemed to be with grace and poise. I was lucky to have Katie as my other sister and now I can't even say goodbye.

chapter 8

MOM MADE IT back and took position at my side. Dad joined us for a bit that afternoon but he wanted to try to work this week while Sara was still in her coma. Dad also stopped by to check on Sara every morning before work and every night after, he did a lot of driving to keep up on everything. Mom helped me brush my teeth and change my gown and helped Mark keep an eye on me. My usual nurse was Mark during the day and he came and went about his business, he did his job well and even though he had to check some of the tubes sticking out of me he still asked nicely and apologized for having to do it.

One day I had a nurse named Kelly Johnson, what a jerk! She made one trip in that day, chewed her gum like a cow with cud and didn't look up from her phone the whole time. Mom mentioned that I was the patient and she just sighed, changed my IV bag and exited. The only way we knew she was a nurse was she was wearing navy scrubs like all the other nurses. This girl couldn't have been bothered to do her job at all. Mom told the nursing supervisor and Kelly spent the rest of my stay on another floor assignment, sans phone.

The first week in the hospital was a dull routine of lying there, getting checked over occasionally, doodle on my laptop and talk with mom a bit when she was there. I knew mom wanted to be in both hospitals with both of her daughters but she stayed with me until I was done eating lunch then made her way to Sara's hospital. I was at Sparrow hospital and Sara at one in Ann Arbor; mom did a lot of driving also. Mom spent most nights with me and dad hung out during the afternoon most days. I felt so bad that their lives were up ended so badly.

That first week drug on, Sara ended up waking up on a Tuesday, one week past Katie's funeral. Mom and Dad were both by her side when she woke up to try to calm her down then explain what all happened. Sara cried so much they said. Mom and Dad spent the first two days with Sara non-stop. I missed them but she needed them really bad. It can't be easy being a parent. I wish I wasn't an additional burden to them right now.

I was visited on and off by different people, one of whom was at moms' request, a therapist, her name was Ms. Rollins. Ms. Rollins was a registered nurse but continued her education to become a therapist also, she told me she was specifically hired to deal with people in my situation, she did it for the patients, and she liked working with kids.

Ms. Rollins sat with me two afternoons a week while mom was with Sara, she asked me a lot of questions about the accident, my life as a child and how I felt about things. I told her that the Kelly nurse was terrible and how Toadstool like I thought Mark looked, she laughed at that one before agreeing. It was nice to talk to her, especially about how bad I felt for mom and dad and the tasks they had before them.

Ms. Rollins explained that one of the agreements parents make when they begin raising kids is that anything that comes up gets handled and that kids always come first, I understood the point she was trying to make but it didn't make me feel any better. I guess Ms. Rollins was requested by mom to help me with the recurrent nightmares of the accident, I thought it was dumb and sure anyone is going to have nightmares this soon after an accident, it'll go away. We spoke about Sara being at another hospital and being in really bad shape and about Katie.

I was really going to miss Katie and it was nice to be able to tell a complete stranger stories about her. I had an hour with Ms. Rollins shortly after lunch twice a week, telling stories about Katie helped me to relive them with her. I spoke about the park and plays, hanging out at the house and of her being there at some of the finish lines at some cross country meets. Katie was really something.

Ms. Rollins asked me a few times about the concert, the afternoon leading up to it and us girls getting all primped and permed. I explained that I chose my cute outfit to be warm and look super cute also. I described Sara's cute boots and how well they went with her outfit of dark jeans and her blouse. I even pointed to Ms. Rollins that my belongings bag was under my bed and that everything was still there. Ms. Rollins pulled everything out and looked at it just like mom did. My white leggings became a focus again and how they didn't end up with all of my belongings.

Ms. Rollins was late during the fourth meeting, Thursdays. Ms. Rollins said she spoke with the on call attending as well as all the nurses that had worked the night I arrived. None of the employees knew about the leggings. The trauma nurse that cut all of my clothes off described what I was wearing and the fashion she sheered them off of me, down to my pink undies and undershirt tank. Ms. Rollins wanted to hear about the accident again.

I spent another long hour describing that we left the concert, all the commotion and laughter and the series of events that I remembered. I lay in bed wondering what happened to the leggings myself. Ms. Rollins concluded our meeting as mom came back to spend the afternoon with me. They spoke in the hallway for a bit, out of range for me to hear and it left me wondering what was going on.

Mom returned from her talk and asked me about my day. Mark came with the dinner tray and checked me over. He asked if I was alright cause he could tell something was on my mind. I just smiled and said I was feeling cooped up as always. Mom and I spoke about Sara; she just got her chest tube out today and endured the fun of being re-wrapped. Sara was still very upset about Katie, like me, she cried a lot. Mom said Sara had a free-ish hand now that they changed her wrappings and that Sara and I could instant message each other.

I was glad that I could talk to my sister finally and I hurried up and logged into my messenger account. "HI sis" popped up. I smiled at mom as she smiled back and watched me type away with my good left hand. I hadn't typed this slow since I was a search and peck typer in third grade. Mom sat quietly in the chair in the corner until it got dark out as I asked Sara how she was doing and how she felt. I told her about Mark and his Mario brothers' entrance music that played in my head every time he came in, it warranted a "lol"

We avoided talking about Katie that first night chatting. Mom asked Sara if she needed anything and was going to head home to check up on our father. Neither of us had any reason to keep her except we were both lonely. It was nice being able to talk to Sara. There were a lot of pauses in our conversation and when she returned each time she apologized that she had been hurting and fell asleep. I wished we were together.

The next morning Mark and Ms. Rollins came in together. I wondered why Ms. Rollins was here, it wasn't our time to chat, Mark did his work quickly. Ms. Rollins used her nursing skills to change my gown and sheets while Mark changed my pee bag. I was due for more bandage changes later in the day and he exited quickly. Ms. Rollins sat in the chair and asked me once again to talk about the accident.

I started telling her about the accident, she asked me to start when I heard the voices of people outside of the car and then when I remember being in the ambulance. I told her about Walker and what he told me. She sat quietly and let me talk but interrupted when I told her about my body lunges and feeling my body lurch against the straps holding me into that bed. She wanted me to keep my eyes closed and think about things beyond what I saw or smelled.

With my eyes closed I spoke about the pains I felt course through my body; my legs pulsed as I recalled the pain while laying there. I told her about that terrible music blaring in my head along with the sirens. I told her about everything blurring as I kept trying to open my eyes. I told her about things dangling and swinging in and out of my view. I was getting dizzy thinking about everything again. Ms. Rollins told me to relax and breathe but that she needed me to keep talking.

We spoke till lunch came in. We kept going over the ambulance ride, she wanted every detail she could get out of me and kept writing everything down. She gave me a strange look when I told her about my legs feeling the cold sheet against them and seeing my feet flopped outside, she said that happens when hips break as the bones aren't attached properly.

I wondered if Sara was getting the same intense treatment. My head felt heavy and the questions left me spinning. My eyes wanted to stay closed and I kept wanting to open them, Rollins just kept reminding me to keep them closed and remember each moment of the ambulance ride. She told me it was normal to swerve in and out of consciousness and that's why I kept having the body lunges that I did.

I guess Ms. Rollins was on to something. I was trying to figure out what she and mom were thinking. I know my missing leggings were at the center of things and why in the world they were missing. I asked what all of this was about and she hesitated for a minute before telling me it was to try to help me sleep better but I knew better. Ms. Rollins was a shorter lady with curly red hair and glasses, I imagined she was in her early fifties and she also bit her bottom lip a bit before answering my question. Mom bit her bottom lip a bit when hesitating looking for an answer, even if it wasn't a truthful one.

Lunch came and interrupted our session which was good. My head was spinning trying to wonder what was going on as well as trying to relive the accident. I was dizzy and tired and wanted to talk to Sara. I did my best to eat, then Ms. Rollins called it a day. I logged onto my laptop after lunch and Sara had left me a bunch of messages, things like; "Hi" "what's up?" "You there?" "What's going on" "Sis?" "HEY" and things like that. I responded and explained I was talking with someone. She asked what kind of someone; hinting at maybe a boy with a winky emoticon, that made me laugh.

We actually spoke about Katie this time. She said she felt terrible about everything and missed her best friend so very badly. I didn't want to ask about the helicopter ride but I asked what she did remember. She didn't remember much, she remembered one or two bits from being in the car and only the noise from the chopper. She didn't remember anything from the hospital until she woke up, casted and full of tubes, how she woke up the other day.

Sara said her ribs hurt like crazy and that chest tube was actually shoved into her ribs, said it hurt like nothing else she had ever felt before. She said her body was sore all over and that she had upper arm breaks in both arms, her right collar bone and her legs were all together but wrapped and bruised anyways. Sara's left arm was slung to her stomach and she was also stuck in one position and suffering from a sore bum too. We both shared smiley faces through our messenger service over some of the wreckage that is our bodies, trying to make light of things.

Sara said mom had arrived and that she'd chat me back in a few minutes. I laid there tired, eyes watering again and my mind wandering. I wonder what Rollins was up to or into, why did she ask so many questions again? Why was she talking to everyone that was involved with my coming to the emergency room? What is going on?

My laptop dinged and I was excited that Sara was back. She said that she spoke with mom for a bit and that mom was headed home for a while, then to see me. I asked her what was going on. Sara told me that mom just had a weird feeling and wanted a lot more answers than I had. I still didn't understand what was going on or why there was reason to be suspicious. I was uneasy about all the hush hushy stuff.

I asked Sara what was going on and why all the sudden weirdness. Sara just said some things didn't sit right with mom and people wondered why. I wasn't getting what she was hinting at and asked her to clarify what was going on. Sara asked me if I was feeling any weirdness in my body, "well sure I was in a car accident dummy" was my response to that particular question. I was getting dizzy after reliving the accident and my head hurt.

I didn't want to stop chatting with Sara and I had missed her all week. I wanted to see mom and was glad she was coming to see me but I wanted her to come see me for me, not because she had some hair stuck in her butt about something. Maybe she felt guilty because she had both of her daughters and Mr. Matt lost his only one. I missed Katie; I could always talk to her when Sara and my mom were being weird. It's getting dark now so dinner must be close by.

I still didn't have an appetite and normally eating wasn't an issue with me. Mark came in and checked up on me before he left for the night. I thanked him for his help and he did his usual empty of my urine bag and had to check "certain areas" to make sure I wasn't getting an infection or anything. I haven't felt right down there since they skewered me with this catheter. I feel like the thing is going to rip something down there, I consider my delicate area well, delicate. I've seen the video of birth, I understand what down there is made for but good god what a blood bath and I have no interest in letting a slimy bloody alien rip through my loins anytime soon.

Mark left for the night and Amber came in shortly after and introduced herself as my night nurse. Amber took my blood pressure and asked how my pain was, I told her it was as it has been all week, enough to be uncomfortable but that the beeping machine over my shoulder didn't help. My legs felt heavy and began to throb again. Amber asked if there was any personal attention I needed, I'm guessing she's hinting towards my monthly visit, I told her I wasn't due for another week or two.

Amber was nice, she had light brown permed hair, bit heavy on the make-up and wore big gold hoops in her ears. Amber was quick in and out before sleep arrived. Mom looked hurried again the next morning and I felt bad that she and dad had their lives completely turned inside out. Mom had a look of intent on her face, I was already uneasy after Ms. Rollins' interrogation followed by an awkward conversation that seemed to be shrouded in secrecy by Sara.

Mom took up her position in the chair to my left again and cleared her throat. Before she could swallow to start talking I asked her what was going on, honestly. Mom dropped her head and said that she had some weird questions and feelings and needed me to remember everything possible about the ambulance ride. I felt my anxiety flare up in my chest and my heart creep up into my throat. I started to shake before she even started to talk. Her silence seemed to last for hours and the wait was almost as intense as the beating in my chest.

What could she be onto? What was going on? Why the big hoopla? Where was dad? The beeping of the monitor above me seemed to scream in the silence of the room. Moms' mouth opened slowly, she started to mutter her first words "we need to talk" then suddenly Mika came in to break the tension and check my bandages. I was glad to see a different face.

Mika was solo as her cohort had to attend to another patient. She was really pretty and gentle as she un-wrapped my legs one at a time. My left leg was easier because it wasn't wired to this high wire looking contraption above my bed. My left leg looked rough as the pins sticking out of me seemed like rotisserie sticks poking into a ham. My left leg hurt but she said things looked like they were improving and that I was healing just fine.

My right leg was her next task. I laid there watching Mika work but my mind was stuck on what mom had to talk about. As the bandages unwound slowly moms' eyes were locked on my mine. I tried to watch Mika work but out of the corner of my eyes I could see mom fixated on my face. My right leg was still lumpy and huge swollen, it was gross looking and the row of stitches running down the center of my knee cap looked like a miniature railroad track.

Mika wrapped my leg, being delicate as she toiled wrapping from my mid shin almost to my private bits. As Mika worked and almost finished up as my anxiety and attention turned back to what mom might have to talk to me about. My heart beat hard and became more rapid. My head was starting to throb. Was I in trouble?

chapter 9

"I THINK YOU were fondled" the words slipped out of moms mouth as she fought back the tears in her eyes. I felt my mouth drop and things became blurry. My head started to spin and it became so heavy. I could feel my chest pound and get heavy into my bed. "What the hell is going on mom?" I just started crying and sobbing. Mom started to cry also. She told me she had concerns that my leggings weren't on me when I arrived in the hospital and that the EMT guy shouldn't have removed them.

Mom told me she had been to the Marshall fire department a few times and Spoke with the Chief whom was on the scene of the accident. The chief described the state of all three victims and what they were wearing as we were pulled from the wreckage that Friday night. The chief told mom that there were three victims in rough shape and once they pulled the truck from the passenger side that the passenger in the back was the first to be extricated (removed). I was the passenger in the back so I was first out because I was the easiest one to access.

Mom told me about how I was removed, tattered and mangled and then loaded into the awaiting ambulance, jean skirt, white leggings, and purple flannel shirt all still on me. Moms concern really sky rocketed when my white leggings weren't in my belongings and no one in the emergency room knew about them. Mom then reached for my bag of bloody clothes and ruffled through them. Mom kept fighting back the tears and asked me if I remember my leggings coming off at all. Once again, I told her I didn't

Mom pulled out my pink undies, cut up each side by the trauma shears in the emergency room. She pointed to the crotch and asked why there would have been some blood smears there. She said she recalls that my "monthly visitor" was two weeks prior to the concert and I felt uncomfortable talking about the subject. Mom apologized a whole lot but she said it was important that I think really hard and focus on my downstairs that night to see if I remembered anything.

All I can remember is the throbbing of my legs and how badly they burned. I remember them being numb and tingling in the accident, the straps squeezing me in the stretcher and hardly being able to see anything under the cloth over my face. Mom said the cloth over my eyes was what seemed weird; there was no reason to have a bandage over my face as there wasn't anything but swelling, no cuts or bleeding. Mom said that when I was telling her about the cellphone I remember seeing also made her uneasy.

Mom continued to talk to me while my head kept spinning. It got heavy and my eyes kept trying to close and my anxiety kept my heart racing which made it hard to be tired. My head kept racing between my cut undies and the tube shoved into me, and then suddenly the glass screams kept piercing the silence between the echoing beeps of the monitor. I got used to the beeping in the background most of the week I've been here but now it's the only thing I can focus on. I hate that beeping.

Mom explained that there shouldn't have been the smear of blood where it was and that there wasn't any blood anywhere else. My head spun more and more. Mom said she was going to stay the night and that I should try to rest because it had been such as long day. Amber came in and mom asked her for something to help me sleep. We sat there in silence for a few minutes, I know mom had more to say and I had so many questions racing through my mind but didn't know where to start.

Amber brought me a big yellow pill and small bit of water to choke it down with. I laid back and waited for it to work but my mind was still going crazy. Mom breathed heavily, I could tell her mind was racing also. I wanted to chat with Sara and ask why all of this was happening. I wish I could just close my eyes, shut my brain off and wake up at home with none of this ever having happened. My heart pounded and my mind darted around faster than ever. Trying to sleep and trying to shut my brain off just made my anxiety worse. I kept my eyes closed but the tears welling up in their corners made it hard to concentrate on keeping them shut.

I laid there waiting for sleep to take over, that peaceful silence that was all calming and removed my control of myself. Minutes seemed like hours and each beep of my monitor seemed to grow quieter and farther apart. I could feel the meds starting to work, my body relaxed and I could feel my body sink into my bed. The hallway lights were a subtle warm pink glow against my eyelids. I liked knowing mom was by my side. It was a big relief having her there.

That night, my dreams kept flashing back to the accident. The growling, crunching of the metal, the screams of the shattering glass overtook all other sounds in the car. The sight of those truck lights coming at us and being trapped in the car, unable to do anything about it, Katie and Sara screaming and coughing. Choking on the smells of burning chemicals and how they made my chest burn with tightness. I felt like I was in the accident all over again.

My dreams suddenly left me strapped in the ambulance again. I was strapped in, feeling cemented to the stretcher with the wailing siren turning into the music from the radio then back to the screams again. It was all a blur and melted together into a dizzying array of sights and sounds that made me so scared. I could feel myself crying but couldn't wake up out of the nightmare once again. I missed my home. I missed my bed. I just wanted to be out of this hell and back to my life, I wanted this nightmare to finally be over.

Mom was holding my hand when I woke up. It was still dark out when my eyes opened. Mom told me it was all ok and that I should go back to sleep. She reminded me she was there for me and that everything will be alright. I was too scared to go back to sleep but my body forced me to lay my head back as things went dark again. My mind raced back and forth between the accident, Katie and the ambulance as well as the emergency room and it all blurred together into doctors and nurses racing around me, cutting my clothes off, having tubes and needles stuck in me and patches being stuck on to me.

I was mostly asleep but I could feel those sticky patches tugging at the skin on my chest. I could hear that squawking monitor beeping in my dreams. The beeping orchestrated some of the screeches from the accident into its chorus of noise. Strobe like flashes of truck lights, the florescent lights flashed overhead when I was being wheeled into the ER, it all was just fast flashes in my head. I felt sick to my stomach then my mind flashed back to vomiting on myself in the ambulance.

Click a sound flashed into my head. *Click* *click* *click* suddenly my mind went to the sounds in the ambulance. The clicking wasn't a metal on metal or the sound of some of the tubes clicking together that I remember seeing swinging in and out of my field of view. The clicking sounded like a camera shutter that I have used thousands of times on my cell phone camera.

I jolted awake, shouting "MOM?" she was still holding my good hand, mom caressed my hair and was trying to comfort me. I felt sweaty and wet. Mom said I had been tossing and turning a bit and was sweating. Amber stopped in to make sure everything was ok and told me that sometimes the medication made people sweat in their sleep. I asked her if it also made dreams really lucid and very real like. I asked mom what else could have happened in the ambulance, she told me that's what she was trying to figure out then asked me why.

I started telling her about the sounds I had heard in the ambulance. I described the cellphone and the clicking sound. She squeezed my hand as I told her and I grew scared. "Oh my god" I remember thinking. What was he taking pictures of? I didn't think anyone actually did that kind of sick thing. Was Walker taking pictures of my beaten body or of certain parts of me? It was getting light outside as I stared out the window.

I was more scared and confused than I remember being while I was trapped in the wreckage. I just laid there, terrified and thinking, everything was spinning in my head. My pillow felt wet and seemed to stick to my head, my hair felt like a nasty rats nest, matted against my head. Mom just stared at me and had a worried look about her. I couldn't look directly at her but in the corner of my eye I could tell she was scared also.

A new nurse, Naiya came in along with my breakfast tray. She introduced herself and said she'd be taking care of me this Saturday. I can't believe it's been two weeks already. Mom was rubbing the sleep from her eyes. I had been awake for a few minutes but wanted to watch the sun wake up the day by myself, and not bother her. She's been kicking her butt running all over. She smiled at me and greeted Naiya. Naiya asked if we needed anything, we did not, and then she left us in our room so we could eat.

I knew mom had more questions; I could see it on her face but wanted to eat with me in peace first. Her uneasy sense of self while eating and helping me to cut my pancakes, kept her sitting on the edge of the chair. Mom ate in sort of a hurry; I ate slowly so I could prolong breakfast before getting to more questions. Naiya stopped in again to put a syringe of something into my IV, she was another beautiful nurse, she reminded me of a cute Missy Peregrym, that actress from that rookie cop show I watched with mom and dad. She looked Middle Eastern and was super polite.

Naiya asked if all of my other nurses were taking care of me as well as I needed and as well as they could. The nurses around here were mostly pretty nice and it was really cool of them to move that Kelly lady somewhere else, I felt bad that I had to complain about her but mom felt like she seemed bothered to have patients at all. The other nurses were very patient, focused and I felt they all took very good care of me. Naiya left to return to her other patients and I was left with the dread that it was just mom and I now.

I loved my mom but I wanted to pretend that this day was over or that none of this ever happened. The loud beep of my monitor interrupted the two seconds of peace and quiet I had in the room. Mom got back to business. "Well" she started. She asked me if I had thought about what she had said and asked what I may have been dreaming about, why it left me sweaty and having bad dreams. I started telling her about my dream. I described the sounds of the camera clicking, the sirens and radio songs that sounded like an angry toddler banging instruments together.

The whole night replayed in my head and I described everything I could to mom. Mom asked about the clicking and if I was sure that it was a camera click sound. She asked where I saw the phone under the cloth on my face and what Walker was saying during any of it. She had me close my eyes and asked me to describe things over and over. My eyes were shut but I could feel my anxiety flare up and my heart throbbed in my throat. Mom stroked my hair and tried to brush my hair with her fingers. I was relieved that she was here but I still didn't want to be.

I opened my eyes and stared out the window. Watching the tree tops sway in the breeze from my window was comforting. I kept thinking about Katie, the memories of her soothed me. I wonder what Sara was doing? How was she? I wanted to grab my laptop and talk to my sister and duck this investigation that mom had going on. I sipped my orange juice, it was nice and cold and very little pulp but it still burned my throat a bit. It is so dry in here, I feel like a piece of human beef jerky, or one of those Mexican cave mummies.

I wanted to go to sleep again, I'm mentally tired but laying here has my body ready to run a marathon. I wanted to ride my bike or jump rope. My legs were still so heavy and my tailbone was very sore again. I asked mom to prop some blankets under my right butt cheek to take some of the pressure off of the sore spot back there. I'm trying to avoid the knowing look mom has on her face. I have so little to do but mom can tell I'm ducking her "look".

I returned to our conversation and retold her about my wet face feeling, the smell of the vomit on my shirt and the collar choking me as I laid there, tied down to the stretcher. Mom wanted me to talk about feeling the sheets on my legs. I told her I remembered lunging against the straps and feeling the squeeze of the straps against my stomach and chest and the cold sheet on my legs. I recalled feeling the pressure on my stomach and everything feeling heavy and squeezing me everywhere.

"*What else happened, what happened to my leggings?*" Do I remember them being taken off or am I convincing myself of something? My head is spinning and I'm getting a headache again. My eyes feel like they are going to bulge out of my head. I'm so tired of crying. Mom still looks so very worried and I wish I could do something about it. What's going to happen with all of this? Is mom going to call the cops? Am I going to be in trouble? Can I just pretend none of this happened? Ugh my right leg is throbbing against the wires keeping it suspended in the air.

Naiya came in and said she had decent news for me, she told mom and I that she heard the surgeons talking that they are considering taking the contraption off my leg in a day or two; oh it would be great to be free of this horrid device and be able to roll and turn over. Naiya had a big smile on her face and it made me very happy to hear that I was on my way to being free and slowly better. Mom was glad to hear that I was slowly making progress as well.

Mom said she was going to head over to see Sara in a bit but that dad should be there now. I asked her what she had planned and what was going to happen. Mom told me that Ms. Rollins was going to hear what I said and then we'd go from there. I had butterflies in my stomach and suddenly the pancakes wanted to make a comeback. I felt queasy and sick. My head was pounding and heavy and I was tired of feeling like butt.

I stared back out the window and wished I was out there, even if I just got to sit outside for twenty minutes I wanted the sun on my face. I thought back to days at the park, singing or climbing around on the big wooden structure, hanging upside down or just sitting on the tire swing with my legs dangling in the wood chips, using my feet to draw as I slowly swung in circles. I guess this is what "winter depression" is like. Mom said she brought some homework for me and that she'd grab it from the car before leaving.

Mom ran to the car and promptly returned with my book bag. I didn't want to do my assignments but I was glad to have something to do. I felt guilty that I had ducked moms' questions but also that she had so many things to worry about. Mom told me that she would be back today if she could but that there were things she had to take care of at home so tomorrow might be better. She wasn't out the door five minutes and I hopped back onto my laptop to get ahold of my sister.

Sara was already on and waiting for me. I cut the chit chat and went right for the center of the issue. Sara asked me some of the questions that mom had asked me, what happened? What I remembered? What happened to my leggings or do I know anything or remember feeling "anything?" I felt uncomfortable thinking about having been touched down there. I didn't want to think about it, the tube in me was still uncomfortable and "it" didn't feel right as it was. Sara said she also had a catheter and it was a terrible feeling.

Sara said she had an influx of nurses hovering around her all the time and it was pretty hard to maintain discretion. I felt better talking to Sara, especially about these private matters. Sara and I spoke all afternoon, she said she was more comfortable talking to mom as dad wasn't one to have conversations with his little girls, especially about intimate things. Sara said she felt like her "plumbing" had been ripped out, shoved back in and not correctly. I laughed a bit to myself.

I felt uncomfortable talking about these situations, but it was a little easier with Sara than talking to mom or Ms. Rollins. It's funny that these talks are so terrible to talk about because all girls go to the bathroom in groups and stereotypical things like that. I always felt more comfortable going in groups because mom and Sara were usually there. Sara said she had to speak with a counselor about what all happened and about the loss of Katie. Sara felt responsible that Katie perished in her car. She understood that it wasn't her fault but still felt awful, it was her best friend that passed away.

I felt my eyes welling up thinking about Katie. Sara said she cried a lot about Katie also. They were best friends since like second grade. I was hardly out of diapers and don't remember actually meeting Katie, I just remember her always being there. Bobbi logged in! Oh I was so glad to hear from her. I talked to Sara and Bobbi for a bit. It was nice conversing and seeing what was happening in the life that I was absent from.

Bobbie spoke of the newspaper article that talked about the accident. The memorial for Katie they held at the high school and the pictures that were up in the halls. Bobbie told me her parents said hi and that they sent their best regards. I dreaded the bag of homework in the chair and avoided that more than the conversation with mom. Sara prodded some more about everything else. She asked me why I ducked talking about ambulance things.

I told Sara I didn't want to talk about a lot and that it was all so overwhelming. I told her my head spun trying to get ahold of all the stuff that happened. Sara was also having nightmares of the accident. She told me that she remembers hearing my screams and Katie's moans. I finally gutsied up and asked about the helicopter. Sara said she only remembers the loud whooshing of the helicopter blades for a few seconds and hardly seeing people's faces. She continued talking about her surgeries and things during the accident.

Sara said she had a cysto something, where they had to put a tube up her urethra and fix a ruptured bladder because it popped in the accident. She was mortified that she had peed all over when the car slammed into the wall. We both laughed a bit talking about how we felt like we had boy parts instead our girl parts because things were terribly swollen down there and each had a tube dangling where it shouldn't be.

She and I compared broken bones and how badly beaten up we were. We agreed that the car accident sucked big time and that the hospitals were nothing like the TV shows. She commented that she had some hot docs wandering around and got a lot of treatment in the intensive care unit she was in. I told her about the pretty nurses and quietly hoping Mark was hit by a big cartoon turtle shell, she laughed pretty good about that. I didn't want Mark to be injured but I'd probably wet myself if he spun out or something like the video game.

chapter 10

SARA WISHED WITH all of her might that she could go out and run. Her left leg had a plate and screws in it like my arm did. She won because she had thirteen screws to my six. Bobbie talked about some of the boys saying that accidents were rowdy and that it was hardcore to have survived one as bad as ours. The newspaper article showed a picture of what was left of the car after they had to cut Katie and Sara out of it. I didn't want to see the pictures.

I wanted to be at home, all of us and Bobbie and Katie sitting around bugging dad about when the food would be ready as he grilled steaks and veggies. I could go for a grilled steak right now, asparagus, bell-peppers; whole mushrooms all topped with pepper jack cheese, oh man that sounds great right now. Sara agreed that she also would much rather be somewhere else, anywhere but in the stinking hospital. Sara said she was due to be moved in a day or two to a step down room now that she was out of her coma.

The cute Hartnett looking resident knocked. I sent a "brb" to Bobbi and Sara and sat up as best as I could. He introduced himself as Tyson and told me his plan of action. I braced myself for what he was going to do and as he worked I fought back the tears as hard as I could. It really hurt but he pulled the wires out of me knee. I squinted my eyes trying not to watch but was also drawn in. He clipped a few of the wires and it felt gross when they slid out of the skin. Tyson had a rough beard, didn't look like he's had time to shave this weekend as he sat and worked diligently on my knee.

Tyson warned me that in a few more days he or someone else from the orthopedic surgery team would be back to remove the staples in my skin. He gave me directions to keep my movements to a minimum as things inside were still delicate and he didn't want me to risk re-injuring any of his handy work. He cutely smiled at his crack but it didn't land on me because my leg was really hurting from the change of movement.

I logged back in and tried to restart my conversations. It was hard to talk much with my leg in pain. Naiya brought my dinner tray and another pill. She told me that the pill would help with the pain but make me sick if I didn't eat first. My appetite sucked but I tried to eat what I could to prevent an upchuck. Sara and I took a break from talking as we were both in pain. Bobbi asked me to talk a bit longer because she missed me like crazy. She had to eat by herself at lunch and missed passing me for high fives in the hallway.

I laid there with millions of things running through my head. Bobbi agreed with me about the terribly uncomfortable fake penis I had, it being shoved into my lady bits and she kept asking questions. I answered as many as I could and I could tell she was truly curious. I avoided talking about the accident when I could, I told her about feeling trapped and having never been so scared in my life. I told her about the smells of the chemicals and laying there in the emergency room, exposed to the world.

She responded in kind to my answers and it was like she was there. It was getting dark out and my eyes kept drifting out the window during pauses in the conversation. My right leg became numb to the pain that had riddled it just a bit ago. I explained to Bobbi that all this pain was exhausting and if I passed out again that I was sorry in advance. Bobbi understood and suggested I relax as best I could anyways.

My body eased from the tension and my head became heavy again. I could feel my eyes start to roll back into my head again. I said goodbye and closed my laptop. I laid there for a few more minutes trying to not think about the accident, I failed. The harder I tried to not think about the accident the more I thought about it. I tried to picture a black chalkboard like at school and that I had an eraser and erased it all and let it fade to black. As the board in my head went black so did my mind.

I woke up the next morning hungry, I was actually hungry. I don't remember sleeping or dreaming, maybe I was free of those nightmares. I got breakfast shortly after waking up and another new nurse was here. Naiya was off for another assignment so now I had Adam as my nurse. I know anyone can be a nurse but it was kind of funny to have male nurses. Adam was an older gentleman and was very kind. Adam said he had a daughter around my age and an older son that was in the army. Adam said I was lucky to be here and that my parents were lucky to have both of their children with them still.

Adam changed my IV bag and adjusted something on my monitor before putting the blood pressure thing on my arm. I asked why I had my arm squeezed so much. Adam told me that they have to monitor my heart rate and blood pressure while I'm on the pain medications. I wasn't sure why but I knew that he had too much to do to answer so many of my questions. He bid me a good morning and reassured me he was just on the other end of the red call button on the remote I had. I forgot I had a TV in my room, I hardly used it.

I logged back on to my laptop when Mika strolled in. She was chipper and smiling pushing a cart. She asked me how I was doing and told me that she was going to pull the staples out of my leg and change the bandages. Mika asked me to remain pretty still and warned me that it might hurt to pull the staples out, she also said that Adam was right behind her to help her clean me up some more.

Mika un-wrapped my right leg by propping my foot up on pillows and made sure it didn't put too much pressure on my knee. My leg hurt but it was tolerable for now. Mika just cut down the side of my bandages rather than actually un-wrapping them. My leg was less purple and greener than it had been and she pointed out that it had meant I was healing pretty well. Mika pulled out some plier looking things and started to clip the centers of the staples. Each click of the clippers pinched a bit and she carefully wriggled the staples out. I felt the pull of the staples and then Mika used a wet sponge to put numbing medication and some orange stuff on the cut.

"God what an ugly scar that is" I said to Mika as I looked at the mess that is my right leg. Mika assured me that with ointment the scar will fade but will leave some marks. Adam came in with a wash cloth and pink square bucket of warm water. Adam started at my foot and cleaned my leg off as Mika unsnapped the staples. The process seemed to take twenty minutes and I kept trying to keep my parts covered as the breeze made me shiver. The wet on my leg was warm but it felt cold as he finished and there was a cold breeze shooting at my girl parts and it was freezing.

It was so embarrassing that I had to pee in a bag and the tube in me made it feel like I always had to pee. Mika made another splint and molded to the underside of my right leg, she said the swelling went down a lot and that this new splint would fit better. Once they were done washing me up and re-wrapping me with new white bandages then the ace-wraps over top. Mika told me that this week I'd start physical therapy to start working my legs and arm. It didn't take long and they changed the wrappings on my arm also.

My right arm looked just as bad as my right leg. The incision site on the underside of my arm was nasty with black stitches poking out. Mika removed those stitches also and said that that scar would heal also. A big machine came in and a tall older guy with a mustache and glasses introduced himself as Chuck. Chuck had an ambitious student with him and they began placing an x-ray plate under my arm and a lead apron over the rest of me. They snapped pictures of my arm and right knee then off they went. The student pushed the big x-ray machine and they murmured back and forth about what all they had to do next.

Once again I was alone and in pain. My right side hurt and I was exhausted. I was so full of energy and after running with Sara I could normally still go play with Bobbi. Just being jostled around wore me out. Pain sucks. I logged back in to see how Sara was. She was just lounging around waiting for time to pass. I told her about my big day and all that had happened. Sara said she has plenty of visiting doctors and nurses constantly tugging at wires and tubes that coursed her body. I felt bad that she was getting poked and prodded more than me but was glad it wasn't me.

I felt better now that I wasn't tied to the bed the way I was. A guy came in to undue the metal frame around my bed and loaded up his cart and moved on. It was me and my laptop again. I chatted with Sara a bit before she had to let me go for her hourly check-up. Sara was still being monitored pretty closely because of her head injury and she got the joy of having lights shined in her eyes. She said she hated that the side of her head was shaved and it felt super weird having the bald patch. She had a brain doc guy named William Godfrey checking on her, she said he was cute but could tell he worked a lot inside; he was "vampire pale" but very personable and took the time to explain all sorts of things to her.

I'm so glad the only thing they had to cut on me was my clothing, I would have died if they shaved off any of my beautiful hair, well it's normally beautiful when it's combed and done, not like this mess I've got going on right now. I was once again alone. Mom said she was running errands today but was going to try to come back to see me this afternoon, I looked forward to seeing her.

I unzipped my bag and looked at the mess of books and homework that stared back at me. I felt tired again and my head was pounding. I put my bag back and laid back. I couldn't really sleep but staring out the window brought me comfort. The swaying tree tops soothed me and I felt my heart rate slow down. I wished Katie was here to just sit with me and watch them with me. I wish Sara and I were free from our bonds and at home.

I watched the trees for a while; the sky remained cloudy but bright with the sun behind them. It looked like a crisp march day but I don't even know what the date is right now. I don't know how many beeps passed as I watched the trees. I don't know how long I stared out the window until the lunch tray came in. I was still so tired and just worn out. I hardly ate again and wasn't hungry. I picked at a few of the fruit pieces and sucked down another glass of water but wasn't up for eating the sandwich.

I wonder if this is what jail is like? Just sitting and waiting for time to pass, staring out the window. My laptop dinged but I wasn't up for talking. I wanted company but I just didn't feel like doing anything. I'm tired and my body hurts all over. I miss Katie. I'm tired of crying and it tires me out but it's about the only thing I can do. My eyes are heavy again. I feel my body becoming tired and my head feels like it's sinking into my pillow again. My eyes slowly close as I stare out the window and watch the trees sway.

I jolt awake with the screaming glass sounds in my head again. I wake up crying and reaching for my bed because it feels like I'm falling. The sudden movement sends pain down my legs and then racing back up to my brain. It's getting dark out but I can hear nurses and people in the hallway. No one is in my room, I'm alone still. I don't feel like talking so I'll leave my laptop on the chair. I rummage through the remote to quickly get fed up of the eight channels, nothing is on. The news is reporting even more violence in the Middle East and people hurting each other again. I'm tired of the noise and shut the TV off again. The talking in the hallway blurs to a dull roar and it's almost inaudible.

My head is heavy and my body has so many pains running through it. My legs throbbed but my right leg felt so much better being free from the sling it was in. Lowering my leg took a lot of the pressure off of my sore hind end. I was able to roll a little and even though it took a lot of work moving pillows to make it happen; it was so worth it. It's sad that I've taken simple movements for granted but moving just a little felt amazing. I couldn't see my tree tops moving and I wanted to watch them. I felt angry that I fell asleep and missed out on more of their motion.

Amber came in to bring me my night pills again and fidget with my blue pump thing. She checked me over and took a look at my fake penis and changed the tape that held it against my inner thigh. I asked her how long I had to have that irritating thing. She gave me the news that I'd have it until I could walk and make it to the restroom myself. I craved a hot bath so bad right now.

Amber checked my vitals and asked if I needed anything with a smile and there wasn't anything I could think of besides the company. I was lonely and the silence was maddening. I didn't want Sara or mom right now. I wanted the company of a stranger, someone that wouldn't talk about the accident or anything that happened. Amber was sweet but I couldn't monopolize her time to much. I thanked her for asking and let her get on her way.

The night toiled away and I just listened to the people in the hallway. I couldn't really make things out but the unrecognizable noise that seemed to fill it was comforting. I missed my life, my friends, school. I actually missed school. I didn't miss the douche bag boys with the popped collars and daddy's money but I missed sitting in a class and the daily mess of classes. I missed meeting my friends at lunch or after school. What would possess a straight guy to pop his collar, spike up his hair with more product than the nearest girl, and fake bake?

And skinny jeans? Boys that's not the right way to get into a girls' pants! I wonder how so many stupid trends become anything popular, Hitler started a fad too and look how terrible it turned out. High school becomes so much worse. Katie and Sara have me truly worried about how brainless and dumb kids get. People putting piercings in their faces and what not, ugh. And neck tattoos? Nothing says "would you like fries with that?" more than a neck tattoo, I mean seriously.

I wonder how Mr. Matt is doing. I miss Katie so much. I feel so horrible about what happened to her. I wonder what it was like. My chest hurt and the tightness was coming back. I hope Katie died in peace and not filled with worry and fright. Did she know what was happening? That she was dying?

The night dragged on as I lay there. The room went dark and someone pulled my door the rest of the way shut. The beeping of my monitor was the only sound I had as company. I think tomorrow is Monday again. I should get my homework done before I get too far behind. I drifted off to slumber to another night of reliving the car accident and all the events that followed. The clicking of a camera shutter made frequent visits to that dream and I couldn't help but to dream of Walker taking pictures of my privates. I tried to fight those thoughts in my dreams but I was prisoner in my dreams.

chapter 11

MONDAY MORNING CAME as the previous had, soiled with the aftertaste of the previous night's vivid dreams. Breakfast came and went and I picked at the eggs and hash browns like a bird. Chuck and Vicki the x-ray techs came in to get updated pictures of my right knee and arm so the doctors could plan my physical therapy coming up. I felt like butt, my body ached and was still sore but my backside didn't hurt as bad now that I was able to roll a little. I was so tired of laying here.

Mark swooped in with his good morning introductions and IV bag change. He also changed out my urine bag and a change of sheets and blankets. Mom came in while Mark was finishing up. Mom reminded me to get on top of my homework and asked how I was so far today. I told her about my dreams and the camera clicking. Mom said she dealt with car insurance nonsense last night and that she wanted to get Sara and me our new cellphones today or tomorrow. I would be so glad to get my phone back.

A tall athletic man came in shortly after breakfast. "John" introduced himself, he was a medium dark man with a clean haircut and camouflage scrubs, the scrubs were pretty cool. John was a physical therapist and spoke to mom and I, he had plans to start working my legs. Tyson came in with a hurry and just like that I was having a party.

Tyson told mom and me that I'd be missing lunch in exchange for a late afternoon surgery to remove the pins in my legs. John and Tyson took up position by the door and discussed that I wouldn't be walking for at least another week but that John would start off with water therapy to work on my muscle mobility. Mom asked how healed my legs would be after two weeks. I guess with my youth I'm healing well but because the femurs are the strongest bones in the body and that they'll need to be babied.

John said that water therapy was basically a hot tub for me to just dangle my legs in for two or three sessions. I will say a hot tub sounds pretty sweet right now. I waited for Tyson to explain that the surgery would be an hour long and I'll end up waking up feeling groggy again in the PACU but that the pins will be gone but I'll have to keep the splints on my legs for a while longer afterward.

Tyson left with a hurried pace again. John spoke with a gruffy Danny Glover like voice, it was soothing and he had a really big smile. John said after a few sessions of stretching my leg muscles that the next sessions would be working with rubber bands to strengthen them. John said by the end of next week I should be walking a bit with help and slowly getting my legs used to walking again.

I don't think I'm that weak; I've only been lying here two weeks or so. Things shouldn't be that bad. John excused himself and said that he'd see me tomorrow after lunch. I was looking forward to getting out of this room for a bit. Mom and I started talking about the therapy and she knew I was nervous about surgery. I don't like the idea of lying in a bed being wrenched on like I was a car.

I asked mom to search my drawer in my room and get me two of my bathing suit bottoms so I could stay mildly covered while in therapy. Mom nodded and agreed that I had a good idea. Mom told me that she was going to meet with a detective to look into the ambulance ride. I started getting nervous and uncomfortable at the idea of being photographed and things like that. What if I was wrong? What is going to happen?

My heart started pounding in my neck and I started getting light headed. Mom could tell I wasn't feeling good and asked me to hold out and bear with her. Mom explained that Walker wouldn't be arrested unless something actually happened but that someone would be by just to talk. I didn't want to keep going over and over what happened. I wanted to just forget about everything.

Mom kissed me on the forehead and told me she'd be back later. She was barely out the door and I was frantically reaching for my laptop. I started messaging Sara and wanted to know what I should do. I was getting scared and my lightheadedness kept trying to force me to take a nap, I can't handle all of this. Sara wasn't responding so I closed my computer and went back to staring out the window.

I had no interest in the TV, there wasn't anything ever on anyways. I was dizzy and tired but not tired enough to sleep. I just wanted my head to stop spinning. The tree tops started swaying a bit and I just imagined Katie was making them dance to make me feel better. I felt my pulse slow down a bit and I became at ease. I had so much whipping through my head. Was I molested? Did Walker touch me? What happened to my leggings and why? Will therapy hurt? Are my legs strong enough to work right? Will I have a limp or anything?

My arm was hurting and it still hurt to move my fingers too. Mark came in and pulled up a stool from under the sink to my right. He said that because it's been over two weeks and that I seemed to be improving that they were going to start reducing my pain meds. I wondered if I was going to start hurting more and why now instead of few days into my therapy. Mark told me that a "sports rub" would really help with the sore muscles after therapy and that the trainers would also do muscle rubs to help. He suggested that I take up the "after workout rubs" and sure it might be weird but that John and Jose were really good at their jobs. I passed a quizzical raised eyebrow and he reassured me that Jose was John's assistant.

Mark sat for a few more minutes to tell me more about the therapy. Mark said his wife Annie had blown out her knee in a marathon and between her rehabilitation and the many of his patients he has seen go through their care that he could reassure me that everything was going to be ok. Marks talk was comforting and I did feel better. Mark let me know that lunch time was around the corner and that I should do better at eating than I have been come dinner. I know I haven't had much of an appetite but with everything going on, my head spun too much for my stomach to feel apt to do its job.

Mark left my room and closed the door behind him. Here I was again alone and bored out of my mind. I stared at my worthy opponent on the chair; I dreaded what was in my backpack. I mustered up the nerve to unzip the beast of a bag and start digging in it. Ugh my e-con book was the first one I pulled out. The subject was a snore and the book was an ugly pea green with pictures of mountains on it. The sticky note on top read "CH. 6-9, problems in the back and worksheet." The adults of this country can't balance a checkbook and like most political parties they figured that they should leave the mess for the next generation to clean up.

E-con was being introduced in the junior high school rather than an optional class in high school. The subject almost bored me to death, supply and demand and China's demand for materials and production of product blah blah blah. I opened to chapter six and started reading. I tried to finish chapter seven before lunch time came. I figured I'd skip the homework problems and read chapter eight as the information was ongoing so I could better do the work by reading ahead.

I was getting kind of hungry and it was about lunch time, of course the day I couldn't get lunch is the day I'd get hungry. I heard a knock at the door and as I fixed myself to receive, it swung open. There were two people entering my room. A tall black man wearing black work pants and a maroon button down shirt, he introduced himself as Azeem and he was accompanied by Sheila, a patient tech. They were here to escort me to the pre-op wing before surgery.

I hid most of my gear; Sheila helped to tuck away my laptop and such within my book bag. We covered me up and headed out and down the hall. I stared at the ceiling and tried really hard to focus on the ceiling. Exit signs, florescent lights and ceiling tiles strolled over me again and again then finally we made it to the elevator. Two giant stainless steel doors opened to greet my escorting party. I was flattered to have the entourage but I really didn't want the attention.

The doors opened to the first floor and we crossed a hallway. Azeem asked the nurse with curly black hair what slot I belonged in and she quickly pointed him in the direction. Azeem and Sheila spun me around and backed me into a small space with curtains enclosing it. The curtains were pastel rainbow colored but thin. You could see the shadows of people pacing back and forth on the other side then a nurse came in. Andrea introduced herself and started asking me a barrage of questions.

"Any chance of pregnancy?" that was the question that made me the most uncomfortable. She followed up with what I've had to eat today, allergies, height, weight and things of that medical nature. Next she had to check my catheter. I took a deep breath and Andrea lifted my gown. I felt a bit of a jostle and she quickly recovered me. She wanted to make sure the balloon was still holding well. *There was a balloon in me? Are you serious?*

Andrea asked me to lie back and relax; I was due in another half hour or so. I listened to people come and go in the makeshift rooms next to me. I had to listen to people moaning and groaning and nurses use terms like vasovasostomy and colorectal biopsy type stuff. All of it sounded not pretty and all I could think to myself was "*god this stuff sounded terrible*". I lay there for a while just listening to the clock ticking on the wall above me and all sorts of monitors, beeping like crazy, it sounded like an arcade in here.

Andrea pulled my curtain back with Tyson hot on her heels. Tyson said hi and made sure I remembered who he was. He quickly asked me if I had any questions as we made our way out. Another lady lifted my head and put something over my hair. That same lady told me that she'd be the anesthetist and was in charge of putting me to sleep. I felt a lump in my throat. It was hard to swallow let alone talk. My stomach growled as we turned a corner. This hallway was intimidating, all white, stainless steel sinks by each door, each sink covered with boxes and rubber gloves draped all over. I could feel my eyes starting to water, I was getting scared.

There was a short nurse standing in the hallway and asked *"is this Lorna?"* Tyson said it was and she introduced herself. "Hi *Lorna I'm Martha Chiplis"* the lady had a blue hairnet on and the grayish blue scrubs that everyone we passed were also wearing. Martha had a smile as big as could be. Martha said she had a reservation for me in the suite right around the corner and grabbed the corner rail on my bed to help steer. As we neared a room Martha said *"this is where the cool cats hang out"* she was funny and cute.

We turned around another corner then right into a room. The room was very scary and the lump in my throat felt like a bowling ball. I couldn't swallow and I started getting dizzy again. There were people in dark green gowns holding their hands up, other people with masks and hairnets on. There were big towers covered with machines and wires; they looked like stacks of DVD players. There were two giant UFO looking lights over top and computer monitors hanging from the ceiling.

In the corner there was a stand with someone sitting at a computer. Against the wall there was a giant half circle machine with giant domes at the ends and the domes were draped in plastic hair net looking things. My pulse was racing and I could feel myself sweating. I could feel myself getting colder as my forehead started to perspire. The people in the room rolled my bed up next to a skinny table that had blankets on it.

The one lady that introduced herself as Martha said she was the charge nurse in the room. Martha was very short and only had her eyes uncovered but you could tell she had that giant smile underneath. Martha was sweet and she explained what I was in for. Martha yelled for a "time out" and my nerves went crazy again. Martha explained that the "time out" was standard to confirm "who was who" and who was doing what.

Martha said she was in charge, Lorna Daniels was the patient, she asked me my birthdate and I told her. She pointed out Tyson and told him he'll be doing the work, he nodded and responded with "yes ma'am" then he chuckled. Martha really was in charge. She had the room laughing a bit as she went around pointing to people and telling them what they were doing. I relaxed listening to Martha go about doling out duties, she went through the x-ray techs and even the peri-op tech Matt.

A familiar voice popped up from near my head, she was Amy the anesthetist again. Amy's head popped over mine and told me that she'll be putting me to sleep and to lay back and relax. Amy placed a mask over my face and asked me to count backwards from one-hundred.

The mask was snug against my cheeks and I felt people start jostling my body. My body was starting to tingle and go numb as I saw my sheets go flying off. Nurses started removing my blankets, I tried to tell them *"no"* and that I didn't want to be uncovered. I felt bare then I heard Martha count from three to one, on "one" my body heaved up then down onto the skinny table. Amy spoke in my right ear to keep counting and I'll be asleep any minute. I felt completely naked, and then my upper torso got covered with warm blankets. Oh those warm blankets were soft and I stopped shivering.

My legs were numb but I could feel my body shake and wriggle as something was happening to them. People were moving my arms and I could hear noises in the background. I could hear packages being ripped open, people counting things. The sound of a drill startled me but I was getting too sleepy to care. My eyelids went heavy and things went dark I could still hear some voices but things melted together into a murmur. The warm soft blankets against my skin and warm sounds in my ears are the last thing I remember as I drifted off to sleep.

Sounds started blurring into my head, it was heavy and pounding. I slowly started feeling my body and my legs began to throb. I felt a tube on my face and my nose tickled really badly. *"Lorna hunny"* I could hear a ladies voice talking to me. There was a lot of noise on both sides of me, it was dizzying. My eyes were heavy and felt stuck together, they didn't want to open.

My eyes slowly opened and tears filled them up, I blinked to squeeze the tears from them and one ran down each side of my face. *"There's our girl"* I recognized the voice from before. I heard a man speak up, *"it's Mike and Janet, do you remember us?"* Mike said. I sort of recognized them from last time I woke up here two weeks ago. Mike's goatee was still trimmed and as white as the hair on the sides of his head and Janet was more awake and smiling than last time in the middle of the night.

My eyes kept rolling to the back of my head and my head was too heavy to hold up. My stomach was empty but trying to empty itself anyways, it rumbled and gurgled. Janet gave me a sip of ice water but that immediately made me vomit. Mike was quick on the draw with a catch basin; he smiled it off and said I was very lady like, "no chunks". His slight giggle made me smile and it reminded me of Dad. I wanted dad to come through the doors again.

I felt the sore in my leg muscles cause spasms and hurt. A short Indian man came and put a medicine in my IV and moved along to another patient. This room was full and had a lot going on. Janet stuck by my side on a stool while Mike hurried about checking with other nurses. Martha came back in to talk to me and Janet. Martha said that everything went well. She proceeded to tell me that they propped my legs up, removed the screws that went into my bones and that I had small holes in my thighs. There were Band-Aids over the holes but that because I haven't been able to move my muscles much for over two weeks that they were going to hurt.

Martha made the suggestion to rub my legs when I could and she had an order in for extra strength sports cream with aspirin in it. Martha rubbed my hand and said I did a great job before she wandered off down the hall. Janet sat with me but suggested I lay back and try to sleep off the medication some more. I closed my eyes but the spinning in my head and stomach got worse. I asked Janet to prop my pillow up more and after she did the spinning got better.

I heard Mike talking a bit later and he mentioned my name. I popped my eyes open to see him walking mom back to my bedside. I was so glad to see her. I felt my eyes watering up as she walked closer. Mom apologized for taking so long and said she tried to make it before my surgery. I understand she had a lot going on even though I would have loved to see her before going under the knife.

Janet moved so mom could have her stool and she took up position next to me. Mom held my hand and asked me how it went. Mom could tell my head was spinning and she kept my talking to a minimum. Azeem and another tech came to take me back to my room. Mom stayed by my side with the exception of turning some corners. I liked having mom by my side right now, I felt like butt again. We made our way back to my room.

We passed the nurses' station and Mark was standing there waiting for my return. Mark joined my small group of people that traveled with me back to my room. Mark helped Azeem and mom get me tucked back into my part of the room under the monitor. Mark reattached my wires to that dumb machine and recovered me with new blankets then said ado. Azeem was right behind Mark on their way out and it was just mom and I left.

Mom told me that dealing with the insurance was a bummer. She told me more about her day and that she checked up on Mr. Matt. Mr. Matt was having a hard time and was missing Katie really bad, we all were. Mom text dad that I was out of surgery and he responded by asking her to tell me "hi" I missed having him around but he had to work since mom took time off to deal with us girls and the hospitals' stuff. I was starving.

Mom asked if I had anymore memories about the ambulance ride and how I was feeling about everything. Mom was having a meeting tomorrow with the sheriff about the investigation. I felt super uneasy again. Talking about this whole deal made me queasy. Mom said she and the sheriff would probably be in early before lunch so I had time to handle everything and still make my therapy appointment with John.

Mom tried to comfort me about everything that happened but it didn't help. I looked at my backpack for a moment then let my eyes wander back out the window. Mom kept talking, but it was a mumble as my attention was trained on the tree tops outside. Some of mom's words caught my attention; she mentioned things such as going back to school and life around the neighborhood. I didn't really catch much of what she said until she mentioned Sara.

Mom said Sara was still struggling and also speaking to a counselor, I didn't mind Ms. Rollins but speaking with her just felt off. I was supposed to open up and spill my guts to a stranger? The whole idea of a shrink wasn't fun. I sat and wondered if anything would happen to Walker? Maybe he didn't do anything and mom was maybe blowing things out of proportion. I can hardly remember a lot of what happened and it was all a blur. Maybe I was wrong?

The night rolled on and I was glad to see the dinner tray. I ate slowly but mom and I hardly spoke. It grew dark out and my legs throbbed on and off into the night. Mom randomly texted here and there as we sat silently together. Mom broke the quiet by mentioning Sara had a longer road ahead of her than I did and that she could use me handling things well as inspiration. I thought it was kind of funny that my big sister, whom I've looked up to my whole life, was going to need me to give her courage, I was honored for the opportunity.

Mom stayed fairly late that night. She knew I had a long day in the morning and so did Sara. Sara had a cat scan scheduled to check the progress on her brain and more tests. I didn't want to see mom leave but I for once didn't mind the solitude. I could see light snow flakes out my window. The flakes shimmered in the glows of the building lights as they fell passed my window. I watched the window until my eye lids closed and shut out the small room around me.

chapter 12

I WOKE UP Tuesday morning and immediately I had panic in my throat. I knew mom wasn't too far behind with an officer to start my day. I had a lot going on and I reached for my laptop. I saw that Sara had left me a bunch of messages yesterday and I replied to them. I apologized that mom had kept me and about my surgery. She logged in halfway through my morning messages.

Sara asked me how I was doing and how I felt. I told her I was super nervous about today. I felt a lot of butterflies in my stomach but they felt more like bricks. Sara told me to hang in there and that she was there for me. My body hurt and the wraps itched like crazy. I wanted a shower and to be able to wash my hair. As the monitor beeped on, the pit of my stomach seemed to keep dropping. I wondered how far the pit would drop before it fell out of me or ended up in my urine bag.

Mark came in to make his morning rounds. The usual chit chat crossed between us and he quickly picked up a few things in my room. Breakfast came in while Mark was still working. I started eating and finished it before Mark was done checking my vitals. I had to lay flat for a few minutes for Mark to check my blood pressure. Mark reminded me that I had my therapy after lunch but that he had a special reservation for me elsewhere in the hospital right beforehand.

Mark exited and shortly after there was a knock at the door. My stomach finally fell out. Mom came in "sweetie" she said. "*We're here*" she warned me. A tall officer followed behind her. The officer was in dark gray pants and a navy blue shirt. It was a state trooper! not even a sheriff. My anxiety flared up like crazy. I took a sip of my ice water from my tray and said "hello" to introduce myself.

The lump in my throat made my introduction squeak out of me. Another sip of water and a hefty throat clear helped me to reacquaint myself.

Detective Williams introduced himself and said he has already spoke with the Marshall fire department chief as well as mom extensively. He had a clipboard and he pulled a fresh page of paper from the bottom then started asking me questions. I retold the officer the events of the accident. I rehashed the ambulance ride over and over. My head felt heavy and my vision blurred on and off having to relive that dreadful night.

My butt numbed here and there and mom helped me to adjust each time. As detective Williams spoke I tried not to laugh as I imagined his dark black mustache looking like a caterpillar wriggling on his upper lip. He was a large built black man and he spoke with such authority and a deep voice that I felt my heart thump with each word. I fought my nerves and the anxiety but I could feel my temples bulge with each answer. I was so nervous and I just wanted to cry. Mom sat in the chair behind me, encouraging me to keep talking.

I spoke about Walker and the terrible radio station noise. The officer asked about what I felt and if I felt anything in my private area. All of this talk and thinking about it made me uncomfortable and I couldn't seem to get settled. I repeated everything that I remembered Walker saying and the things I saw and felt. I spoke of my legs burning and feeling like jelly. I spoke more about the cloth on my face and my entire body seizing on and off.

He stood solid like a wall, he didn't sway or hardly move the entire time, he just kept writing. I felt like there was a giant spotlight blaring at me. I felt so on the spot and I wasn't liking the attention. Officer Williams repeated a few of my details to clarify what he had heard and the muscles on his face let up when he could tell I was uncomfortable. His booming voice seemed to cause my heart to beat harder and it was intimidating but the corners of my mouth seemed to crack because it almost wasn't real.

My head felt heavy and mom petted my left hand. I could feel tears stream down my face as I described every detail of having lay in that stretcher and feeling my body ache. I was tired of having to relive that hell. Williams mentioned he knew the department manager of the ambulance company and his next stop was to go and speak with her. Williams mentioned the next person on his list of people to speak with was Ms. Rollins and asked my permission if he could.

I granted him the right to speak with anyone he wanted to. I hoped I wasn't getting anyone in trouble. I wanted mom at ease but I knew this lump in my throat was only going to get worse. My temples throbbed, my heart raced, I could feel my armpits perspiring, and needless to say I was really uncomfortable. Detective Williams finished up his interviewing on my end and said that he might be back later in the week if he had further questions. I didn't really want to see him again, he was a nice guy but I wanted to close my eyes and cry all of this away.

The detective shook my hand and thanked me for my cooperation. Mom escorted him out of the room and spoke with him a bit longer outside the door. His voice was so deep that it seemed to echo in the hallway but the bass it held made it hard to make out what was being said. The lunch tray came in and mom shortly to follow. I was starving and really glad that the interview was over. Mom asked me what I thought about the whole ordeal. I explained my extreme dislike towards everything.

Mom apologized about my leggings going missing but it really raised a flag with her and she had to know what happened. Mom said she couldn't stay much longer because she wanted to make it to see Sara and the almost two hour drive sucked. Mom also mentioned that our new phones should be ready later today and that being able to text back and forth would be a huge help. Dad worked for a Michigan mortgage company as the head underwriter so it was really hard for him to take much time off. Mom explained that he said hi and sent his love each time and felt terrible that he couldn't be with one of his girls but he also was spending afternoons with Mr. Matt.

Mark stopped in and said that I had an appointment coming up before therapy and asked if I'd be ready to go in twenty minutes. Mom finished up our brief conversation and told me she'd be back in the morning. Mom gave me a big hug and she could tell by my hug that I didn't want her to leave. Mom helped me into my bathing suite bottoms and tied them the best we could manage. The suite covered me enough but with the tube dangling out of me it didn't fit all that well. She said she was so sorry but that she had to go. I really did understand but a part of me really wanted the attention, and the company.

Mark came back and helped me pack up to go. Mark was smiling and telling me that we had an hour stop off of the fourth floor. The fourth floor was more of a senior rehab floor and that there was a specific room there that had an opening for me. Mark had a smile on his face and he looked ever more like toadstool. Mark said usually they'd transfer me to a stretcher for moving but because I was still a mess and mummy wrapped that leaving me on my bed would be easier.

We strolled down the hallway and Mark just kind of hummed to himself. Mark mentioned that he pulled this favor for me so he'd take me himself rather than let some of the patient transporters in on his secrets. The elevator doors opened up the fourth floor. We made two right turns then a left and there was a room with two big windows to it. Mark parked me out front and walked in. Mark came out and told me that Sally was waiting; he reassured me that he had told mom what he had done and thought I could use some special attention.

Sally came out. Sally had short blonde hair that was sort of spikey and blue eye shadow. Sally wore a green work shirt and had bright fun socks that came up over her pant legs. She made the bed bump twice as she unlocked it, then Maria, her sidekick, came to help. Sally introduced herself and Maria then told me Mark had bargained a sweet salon package for me. I was very glad to hear that and I'll have to remember to thank Mark so very much.

It was very thoughtful of Mark to make these arrangements for me. I guess its things like that that make him a good nurse. Sally and Maria worked diligently to get me situated into a special chair, they had a beefy guy help move me from my bed and then they got to work. I got my hair washed then brushed, Maria worked on a pedicure while Sally gave me a sponge washing then Maria unwrapped my legs. Both ladies were gentle and got to work shaving of my legs. I had my own small room so it was very personal. Both of the ladies were gentle and it felt so good to be thoroughly cleaned.

I was given a rag to clean most of me but Sally helped me reach areas that I couldn't. Maria helped hold me up while she washed my back and shoulders. I felt so much better and I'll admit I wasn't ready for therapy to start; honestly I wasn't ready for the spa treatment to be over either. A salon in the hospital for patients was a genius idea; I need to remember to write a very nice thank you note.

Both Sally and Maria toweled me off and rewrapped my legs. It hurt my leg muscles a bit when they sat me up but it also felt pretty good to be free of wraps and have the light massaging that came with the washing. Both ladies were very gentle and did an excellent job, I felt so clean now. Maria ducked out of the room for a minute and came back with a small pink bag for me. I was beyond touched that they took such good care of me. The bag contained a small can of spray deodorant, (which was well thought out), a brush, a few powders to help with the itching, chapstick and a small pouch of baby wipes, cucumber and melon scented at that! It was so awesome.

I was rewrapped, packaged up and ready to be delivered to John and Jose at my therapy session. I was kind of nervous. I felt pretty relaxed and didn't want a work out. I wasn't ready for my legs to hurt anymore. Sally and Maria walked me out and we all said our goodbyes as a patient transporter came in and helped them relocate me onto my bed. We headed down to the second floor and snaked our way to a back hallway. I saw John standing by the doorway to greet me.

John asked how I was and I replied that I've had a long day. We wheeled back to a small room and he said I had to change. He had a red half gown that was a lot smaller than the giant one I swam in for the last two weeks. I was nervous about this "changing" he had in store. His gravelly voice was calming but it wasn't enough to settle my nerves. My heart started to pound a bit.

John helped my left arm out of the sleeve hole but stopped and asked me if I could wrangle the gown off over my right arm then get the gown back over my right arm and on. His plan seemed easy enough and surprisingly I was able to manage it. I felt uncomfortable lying there mostly naked as I worked the gown off of my busted arm. It hurt a bit to move and make this change happen. I got the new red gown on over my right arm then worked my left arm into the sleeve hole. This gown was smaller than the other one and it was slimmer in the arm holes. The neck of the gown got hung up on my chest but I'm not well endowed so a slight wiggle and I was home free.

I called for John and he opened the door slowly asking if I was ready for him, he wheeled me out and shouted for Jose. *"Rapido"* he shouted with a smile, a short stocky Hispanic man came jogging along, he had a short trimmed goatee and a crew cut style hairdo. Jose introduced himself and he helped John move me to another room. Jose sounded like he was in his mid-twenties and had a very slight accent. John and Jose busted each other's chops and bantered back and forth. John referred to Jose as Speedy Gonzales and Jose responded with *"Relax Obama"* they were very funny.

Jose and John helped to lift me onto a small chair that was made of PVC piping. Jose spiked John with *"slowdown Will Smith, don't be such a bad boy"* but John quickly hit back with *"hey Luis Guzman, I'm the Count of Monte Cristo here, you're the sidekick"* their friendly harassing was very funny. They un-wrapped my legs splints and my arm making sure I stayed pretty still. I was seat belted into this chair and then they lowered it to its first notch so my feet were in the water.

The water was hot but it felt good. Jose asked me to just flex my feet and make circles in both directions. I made circles for a few minutes then they moved me two more notches. I felt like the chair was going to flip forward dropping me face first into this little tub but John comforted me that he had a good grip on the chair. I was now knee deep in the tub and still making my baby circles with my feet. Jose told me to start gently moving my legs back and forth for a minute or two.

John piped up and told me to start using my moves. He then noted that he had moves like Usher. Jose quickly interrupted and asked if I minded if he "smoked'. I had a look of disbelief that he even asked me. He followed with *"A movie theater usher … BOOM smoked you sucker"* We all laughed and John high fived Jose for the good rip.

John was still chuckling when he asked me to move like I was skating, up through the middle and outwards. He explained that this would stretch the outer thigh muscles in my legs. Those muscles he mentioned started to really burn. I felt my face tighten as I fought back a grimace. All I could do was close my eyes, Jose told me that it was ok and to take it easy a bit. Jose squatted to my left and held my good hand. Jose told me they were going to lower me in further and it might burn a bit more but that I needed to extend and contract my legs.

I sunk lower into the tub and sure enough it burned. Jose squeezed back as tight as I squeezed his hand and he whispered *"fight it girl"* John piped up again; *"What do you know about fighting? NACHO LIBRE"* you could hear him laugh as he spoke in a silly manner. Jose didn't wait very long, as I opened my eyes I saw him lick his teeth under his lips, crack a smile and rifle another worthy shot back to John. *"Well if you want to wrestle its NACHO place and you better LIBRE me alone or you'll be like Eddie Murphy and put out a special of your own, RAW, the story of Johns butt!!"* At this point we were all laughing pretty hard and the pain in my legs subsided a bit.

Jose wiped a tear from his eye and returned to asking me to keep sweeping my legs around in the warm water. I decided to speak up with my own comment and tell them that this wasn't the spa treatment I ordered. John laughed while Jose had a bit more of a sincere look on his face. My suitors were goofy and very easy to get along with but all this moving was really making my legs hurt. Jose told me I've only got about ten more minutes of this workout then they'd get me out and dry me off. I was waist deep in the tub, with the jets turned up; there were a lot of bubbles. Jose wiped his brow on the sleeve of his black scrubs and he bore the heat with me.

I felt kind of bad that Jose was getting splashed by the bubbling water. He just kept wiping his forehead off on his shirt sleeve and kept telling me to keep going. John kept steady grip on the chair I was strapped to then he raised me up. I was dripping wet sitting there and my legs hurt like crazy but in a sort of good way. Jose ran and grabbed some towels then he and John got to work toweling me off. I used my good arm to dry off my gown and wipe my face off. Once dry; John rolled me back into my holding room to change.

I struggled to get the wet gown off of me and was cold so I hurried to change back into a dry gown. Jose knocked on the door and let me know he was waiting to take me to my next stop. Jose then rolled me into another room across the main one and towards the corner. John had a table laid out with fresh white towels on it. John was standing firm with his feet shoulder width apart and his hand over one another. John smiled and in his Smokey voice he told me that the massage portion was next.

I wasn't sure I was up for much more today. The pain in my legs started to make me tired. My thighs ached and my calves didn't feel hot either. I felt flush from the hot water and was getting cold from the air. John said that they had warm blankets for me once I was on the table. Jose parked my chair and then moved towards my feet. John towered behind me and asked me to cross my arms the best that I could. Jose grabbed my feet while John stuck his hand under my armpits and together they lifted me to the table.

It took a minute to get comfortable and the guys placed rolled towels under my head and behind my knees. The towels were soft but weren't a pillow. My hair was a bit wet from the tub and it was cold as it pressed against my neck. John and Jose each took a leg and rubbed the muscles in my thighs. Each squeeze felt like a vice grip on my leg. Johns big hand could almost wrap around my leg while Jose' hands worked faster. I didn't like having two men rubbing my legs, Here I am laying on a table in a flimsy hospital gown and two clean cut grown men massaging my legs, it was abnormal and I'm wasn't thrilled it was happening to me.

I was appreciative for the attention; the limited movement was much desired. I was too insecure to really enjoy the massaging, and "enjoy" wasn't even the right term. I tried not to cower from my caretakers but I was cold, had damp hair, and shivered mercilessly. I tried to focus on the ceiling above me while the men rubbed down my legs and tried to loosen the knotty muscles. I tried to avoid thinking about my still wet bathing suit shorts and how exposed I still was. I hated being displayed to the world like this, even in the small room I was in. The men finished up and put me back as I was when they found me.

Patient transport was waiting for me after I was rewrapped and scooted onto my hospital bed. I rolled through the hospital, on to the elevators and back to my floor. I was chilly but glad to get back to my room. I was rolled back into my room; Mark was once again there to help me settle in. Mark moved my chair close so I could reach my bag and my laptop and off he went.

I opened my laptop and both Sara and Bobbi were on. Bobbi told me about the school day and we chatted about how busy my day was. Sara was still feeling nauseated and dealing with the nasty taste in her mouth that the scan seems to leave. I felt bad that Sara had a rough day and we talked about it a bit. Her CT techs were Jill and Mary and both were very nice to her. Ms. Rollins knocked on my door and asked if it was a good time. I let Sara and Bobbi go for a bit and welcomed her in.

Ms. Rollins told me about meeting with Detective Williams, she said he was a handsome man and was very curious about what she had thought about us and our talks. I also asked her what she thought, both personally and professionally. Ms. Rollins started telling me that there were many things that were suspect and that there were many details that I couldn't have made up but also many that were missing. I guess I spent more time talking and not enough listening during our time.

Rollins and I spoke back and forth for some time. She was still very curious about the events that took place during the ambulance ride, as was I. It all seemed to cloud my mind and it became hard to concentrate anymore. I just wanted all of this mess over. Ms. Rollins started telling me that she felt something happened and that I wasn't letting myself remember. She told me that on Thursday we would go into it further but it was getting late and then she departed for the day.

I laid my heavy head back and took a deep breath. It had been a long day and I was exhausted. It started to get dark again and I hoped the dinner tray was headed my way soon, I was starving. Another knock at the door caused it to slowly creep open. It was mom again. I smiled at seeing her but I could hardly lift my head. Mom told me I looked really tired and asked if I had eaten yet. As she finished her question the dinner tray came in.

Mom helped me eat and we spoke about the day's events since she left earlier. I told her about John and Jose goofing off and being super funny. I told her about my spa deal and the amazing treatment I received. Mom was glad I had a good day and still apologized that I had to deal with the detective. Mom reached into her purse and told me she had two things for me.

She handed me a new phone, all the contacts and most of the text messages had been transferred over so I could get caught up. There were hundreds of messages that I would tend to later. The second item in her bag was a book. She told me Mr. Matt wanted me to have it. It was Katie's favorite book; "3rd Hand Ranch". It was about a group of young girls that each had their own struggles in life and found the inner strength to persevere. Tears started to fill my eyes again. I missed Katie so much, I loved it.

chapter 13

THE NEXT FEW days came and went. Most of my time Wednesday was filled with talking to Sara and homework. I felt so far behind but I had plenty of time but not enough motivation to get it all done so I picked at what I could. Thursday's therapy was another one of being dangled in the pool and John and Jose ripping each other for my amusement. Jose made remarks like *"OOOH Shaft you a bad mamma jamma"* with John returning the harassment with Oscar DeLaHoya comments. You could tell they were great friends but they were sure funny about it.

That Thursday was another grueling one. I was left sore again from my time in the tub. Ms. Rollins came in for another session and this one was extremely difficult. I was asked to lay back and this time she used her notes from my initial night and walked me through the accident then the following hours. Ms. Rollins spoke softly and had me fill in the blanks the best I could. I remembered new details including one that felt like my leggings being cut off of me as well as very disturbing feelings of maybe being touched in a bad way. As our session wrapped up I was crying so hard with the thoughts of someone pulling aside my underwear and the cold I felt on my skin. That night left me with worse dreams than ever and I couldn't shake them.

I told most of this to Sara via text cause it was easier to manage than my laptop. I kept in touch with some of my other friends as well as both mom and Dad. Mom already suffered enough of what I had so I didn't divulge much of the new information to her. My nurses rotated through and even with limited abilities they did their best to take care of me. I wanted out of this place more and more as the days went on. I spent a lot of my time staring out the window and watching the tree tops that Katie made dance for me when I was down.

That Saturday marked our three week anniversary since our accident. I told Sara she cheated by sleeping through the first week. She didn't find it as sickly funny as I did, but in this mundane place I struggled for laughs when I could get them. Mom made her rounds as she did. Dad came in on that Saturday. I was very happy to see him as he couldn't make many of the trips with working and all of the additional tasks he had taken upon himself so mom could keep up with us. Dad had great news for me. Dad said that in the next week or two I would be a free bird.

I was thrilled at the thought of escaping but my joy was quickly extinguished that I would still spend another week or so at home before being strong enough to go to school. Dad also told me that arrangements had been made for an outpatient rehab clinic for me at the hospital in Jackson so we wouldn't have to travel outside of the city to keep up on my exercise. I was still very glad to have the ability to go outside and feel the sun on my face. Dad also pulled out from behind his back a shamrock shake.

I didn't even realize it was St. Patrick's Day and I longed for these shakes all year long. It was so smooth and minty. I lost a lot of my lust for fast food when I was still little, but these shakes were liquid heaven. Dad and I caught up a bit while I enjoyed this giant green cup of goodness. The little ice bits inside nicked my throat but I couldn't stop sucking it down. Dad mentioned that mom was debating going back to work part time and with all the running, bills were piling up. Dad and I spoke about the house feeling too quiet and empty without his little girls making a racket.

I prayed silently that dad didn't bring up the Walker situation; I really didn't want to talk about it let alone with my father. Dad said he had been spending a lot of his afternoon time in the garage wrenching on the mustang and he did it with Mr. Matt. Mr. Matt was still struggling to deal with Katie's death. I couldn't imagine how hard he was dealing with things. Dad told me Katie looked so beautiful in a white satin dress, covered with lace. Her hair combed back and a pink ribbon tying it back. He said it was really hard to watch them close the lid on the casket and everyone that filled the church during the service cried.

Dad also seemed misty eyed just recalling the funeral. Mr. Matt wore a very nice suite that dad took him out to get. "Every man should dress their best in a time like that" he said. I missed Katie more and more as we spoke. I sunk my head into my pillow and kept wishing I could close my eyes and make all of this go away. Dad cleared his throat and then swallowed hard. "There's one more thing we need to talk about" he uttered. A lump appeared in my throat, his words karate chopped me in the neck and I gasped a large breath.

"I spoke with the detective" his words turned to a fist and then punched me in the gut, I couldn't speak. Dad told me that the officer had confiscated the scratched cellphone and there were unfortunate pictures on it. He asked me if I would be up to looking through them and being able to identify if any of them were of me. I couldn't breathe. My eyes started to water. I was embarrassed that my dad was talking to me about my privates and mortified that there was even reason to worry. I felt so violated. I wanted to sink into my pillow and die.

Dads' words blurred in and out and I really fought to hear him. Dad said that everything was going to be ok and that I shouldn't worry or let it bother me. "Whatever happened; happened and it's not your fault" he said. I didn't for a second blame myself but it didn't stop me from feeling dirty and ashamed. I wanted to throw up but I didn't want to waste my cold treat and heaving it up would be a shame. What kind of low life would do such a thing? Dad mentioned that there was a Fred Philps that was scout leader he knew when he was younger.

Philps was a very religious guy but he was found to have a "certain fondness" for little boys dad said. Dad said his best friend Richie was a victim of this monster and what Philps had done changed his life forever. Dad told me that he raised strong girls and that there wasn't anything we couldn't get through. Dad told me that whatever happened from here on out that he and mom would be behind me but this piece of trash needed to pay for what he has done. Like Philps, some of the people in this world were wired differently and being "low life scum" they prey on innocent people and take advantage of them, to be able "prey on" those around them.

Dads speaking didn't help. My head spun and my eyes rolled backwards into my head as I fought the urge to pass out. Dad said that Fred was a leader in the community for a while but that it was all a veil to mask what he was really doing. Fred set himself up in a position of trust and that even if someone means well it shouldn't be an excuse not to use your own judgment. Dad understood that my judgment said to get this dirt-bag but that I was so scared and it looked like an impossible task. Dad said he knew a lawyer from work that we could talk to and that the lawyer would be a mean junkyard dog to eat at this a-hole but also make sure that I was kept safe.

I really didn't know how to feel and the urge to toss my cookies was still very in my stomach. Dad started to pack up his things but he needed me to think about one more thing while he was gone; "What if it happened to Sara, Katie or any other girls if you don't help stop this nonsense?" His words cut deep with sincerity. Dad was right but it didn't ease my stomach.

I felt sick and laid there as he hugged me, then kissed me on the cheek. I didn't want him to leave as he pulled the door shut behind him but I wanted the quiet to think.

I texted Sara and asked her what she knew. Sara reluctantly responded that she knew a lot more than she wished. She said she was so sorry that all of this happened and felt very responsible because she was driving. Sara said it was partially her fault that her best friend was dead, that her sister was in the hospital, that she was in the hospital and that all she could do was lay there and feel awful.

I felt terrible about so many things. I felt bad that Sara felt bad, I felt bad about my beat up body. I felt bad about the events that might land someone in jail. I felt bad that I had to rely on people to help me use the bathroom, for crying out loud. Lunch came in and I really wasn't hungry, especially after the shake followed by the crap news. I just picked through some of the fruit and veggies but the sandwich certainly wasn't convincing me to eat it. I stared at the window until the lunch tray went away. I kept talking to Sara and sent Bobbi some messages but definitely didn't share any of my new situation.

I laid there and fought to keep my mind clear but everything shuttered into my mind and I couldn't fight any of it. I felt myself fall in and out of sleep but each time the glass screams and shrieks of the accident violently woke me up. I felt myself sweating from the lucid dreams so I gave up on trying to rest and got back to my books, and my phone. I kept reassuring Sara that none of this was her fault and as long as she was still my sister I was hers.

I watched the sky turn dark with an orange hue to it, it was so pretty and being the middle of March now spring wasn't too far off. I wonder if it was getting warmer yet. I wanted to be out on the back porch at home, in a hooded sweatshirt and a book in hand while the birds chirped and the sun shone on me. I'm so tired of being stuck in here and tired of lying on my sore butt.

Naiya came knocking in, I was so glad to see her. Her hair was pulled back into a high ponytail and she was happy to see me as well. Naiya told me that she rotated floors but picked up this night so she could get caught up on her own work and check in on me too. She said I reminded her of her little sister back home in Cali and asked me how things were going. She seemed pretty giddy and we began to swap chit chat.

I smiled as I told her about my therapy guys and she laughed because most of the hospital liked those two. Naiya could tell something weighed heavily on my mind and she nudged me to open up. I reluctantly told her about the investigation and what's been going on. Her expression made me feel pitiful. She had a look of sadness and disbelief on her finely shaped eyebrows and she placed her hand on mine.

I sat quietly and Naiya told me that crappy things happen to a lot of people but they are only as crappy as people let them be. I raised an eyebrow and wasn't sure how she meant. Naiya explained that as a nurse she has seen all sorts of terrible things happen to people and the best thing she ever saw changed her life.

One year there was a terrible accident and she was rotating through a pediatric ward. There was a young boy in an accident and he lost his lower right leg when a drunk hit his moms' car, with them in it. She spent weeks assigned to helping the little boy and he was so sad about his mom's car. The little boy had giant dimples, short curly black hair and a giggle that would light up any dark room. Naiya said the boy was almost four and made up words as he tried to read his upside down picture book to her, always a different story.

Naiya told me that she wasn't really supposed to talk about other patients but that I had to hear this story. The little boy sat and read to her one day and she asked him how he felt about his missing foot. The little boy didn't even think before responding "it's ok, I have one good one, and they told me I can get a robot one put there, plus it's one less shoe my mommy has to tie" Naiya said she smiled through the tears but that she has never cried so hard in her life, but it also opened her eyes that things are only what you let them be. Naiya made me cry with her story and I realized that the little boy had a larger view on the world around him than so many angry, closed minded other people.

I wish I had the heart to tell myself that I won't be scared, that I won't consider backing down, that I am made of steel and can do it all, but I'd be lying. I don't know what the heck is going to happen, all I do know is I'm tired of my head spinning and my stomach convulsing with this crap. Naiya came and went as she had to check on other patients and when she was gone I kept tabs on Sara. Sara was readying for her start in physical therapy this week and wasn't looking forward to her tasks either, I just told her she can either be a victim to it or a volunteer to it and take that bull by the horns.

I stayed up late just shooting the breeze with Naiya, she was so sweet to keep me company and so smart about so many things. She told me she was going to let me get some sleep and left for the night. My heart thumped and my mind raced through the days' events. I told myself I wasn't a victim anymore and I thought about that little boy; sitting in a hospital bed, picture book upside down, giant smile and pointing to make up a creative story. He wasn't scared, nor am I, anymore. I dealt with the flashes of memories from the accident that night, visions of the shattered glass, the strobes of sirens and all the chatter. I fought the idea of someone touching me. I shook my head and said "no".

I didn't sleep that well but I really haven't much in the past few weeks as it was. I spent Sunday doing more homework, Math, science, history all the usual subjects. I toiled away for most of the day only breaking to send a return text or eat. I denied needing to see mom or dad so neither came out. Mom spent most of the day with Sara but checked on me a few times through texts.

I wonder if most baby birds don't know if they can fly until they are kicked out of the nest. I woke up Monday morning thinking of that question. I kept trying to stay up on my homework and I asked Bobbi to get the weeks assignments after school for me. I felt a sense of focus and I wanted to get my body back. I got a lot of my homework done between breakfast and lunch. Mark brought me a bag of baby wipes so I could semi bathe. I got frustrated hardly being able to reach everything I needed to with my left hand.

Mark came back in once I was done and he leaned me forward to wash down my back. I let out a big sigh of frustration and he just told me "It's usually the weaker people that ask for help, but it's also some of the strongest that take it" I don't know if he was being funny or philosophical but I was really starting to find my inner strength. Mom text me and warned me that Detective Williams was going to come and see me this week. I reminded her that Wednesday was clear on my appointment calendar, landing me an "LOL".

I stared back at the trees and tried to imagine what lie in store for me. How bad was it going to hurt walking again? What was I going to do when I got home? Mom warned me that at this time I should get used to sleeping on my back because once I chest up, sleeping on my stomach wouldn't be comfortable. My chest itched and I took that as certain monthly things were right around the corner for me.

It was quiet in my room after Mark helped me finish my "bath". I appreciated his help and he was very respectful. I was insecure about my body and I tried not to avoid his touch. It was weird being babied and I still would rather do things myself. I wanted a shower and a bath; I wanted all of my pink fluffy towels at home and my bed. I wanted to walk around and feel the carpet under my feet. I wanted to make foot fists on the soft carpet. I wanted to barge into Sara's room while she was on the phone talking about boys and watch her freak out.

I wanted to ride my bike around the neighborhood. I wanted to walk the crowded hallways at school. I didn't want to sit in class and stare out at the playground; I wanted to be *AT* the playground. I had so many things I wanted to do, but first I wanted out. The idea of being free again had my heart lift. I was excited about the idea and it made me smile really big.

I watched the trees dance more and smiled knowing it was Katie running her hands through them for me as mom ran her fingers through my hair when comforting me. I really missed Katie and her spirit for life. I told myself I would be stronger and live my life the way she would, ready for any adventure and not to back down.

chapter 14

MONDAY CAME AND went and the busy work of Mark kept him occupied. I really didn't have much to keep me company other than my school books and the occasional messaging back and forth with Sara. Sara wasn't liking physical therapy and said she was pretty sore and tired from her workout. Sara said she wished she had my physical therapy guys to make her laugh but she was stuck with two large guys that just seemed to move her around and grumble.

Tuesday started off a good time. I looked forward to my exercise time but not my time with Ms. Rollins. Physical therapy was another laugh session mixed with pains from the work out. Today's session had me hobbling down some parallel bars and slowly convincing my legs to walk as they had for so long before a month ago. My left leg dragged a bit behind me and my left arm took most of my weight while John held me up on the right side.

Jose continued to own John in the insult competition. John called Jose "Gabriel Iglesias" for trying to be a comedian while Jose called him a product of "George Washington Carver's" work, *"Peanuts"*. The guys' volleyed comments back and forth had kept me laughing through the pain. I asked them how long they had been friends, Jose said it all began when John had a crush on his sister, John snapped back that Jose only had a brother, Jose followed up with *"told you"* and more laughter erupted among us. I spent the last ten minutes in the tub before another quick leg rub down, I was shaky being lowered into the water because this time I went without the white and blue chair.

I sat there cooking like a crayfish, flexing my legs in and out to stretch and work my thigh muscles, they ached pretty good and though it felt good to be free from the itchy wraps and splints I knew I had to be careful with them for a few more weeks. I made it back to my room again and lunch was already waiting. I was always hungry after the workouts and Mark told me it was my muscles healing and growing. I scarfed my food and then waited for Ms. Rollins with hesitation.

Ms. Rollins came in half an hour later and with her followed Det. Williams. Williams had his clipboard with him and also his stern facial expressions. I was suddenly really uncomfortable again. The lump in my throat and the heaviness of my belly seemed to all tense up with my racing heartbeat. Rollins started the conversation with telling me the latest on the investigation and that the detective had some questions for me. I really couldn't get comfortable and no matter how I sat; I wasn't going to change it.

Detective Williams removed a scratched up orange cell phone, the same one I remembered seeing in my view a few times in the ambulance. My vision blurred as he turned it on. He said he confiscated the phone as soon as he met Walker. He told me the guy's name was Walker B. Chaudry and he had been an EMT for a little over two years. I really didn't want to know anything about him. Ms. Rollins told me that mom was on her way also.

I was getting even more nervous to add mom to the mix. The detective stood tall and stoic as he scrolled through the phone for a moment. Mom knocked on the door and let herself in. Ms. Rollins and officer Williams greeted her as she made her way to my bed to give me a hug. Mom could hear my voice quiver as I said her name, the lump in my throat had complete control over me.

Detective Williams, tall, dark, broad shouldered and rowdy looking, spoke up and told me that he needed me to look through the phone and the pictures to see if I'd recognize anything familiar. My eyes blurred and I could feel them welling up. I swallowed hard, I'm tough enough for this, and "I can do this" I repeatedly told myself. Ms. Rollins moved towards the foot of my bed and let me know that whatever happens will be trivial and that I could get through anything. Mom rubbed my shoulder and encouraged me to go ahead.

The officer placed the beat up phone in my left hand and I started clicking and scrolling through with the trackball. The trackball felt smooth in parts, worn down from heavy use. The first picture I saw was of a smashed red car, the front end peeled back like a banana. My nerves raced my heart beat as each picture passed, it was hard to figure out which was faster. My eyes were wet but my mouth dry; I don't get how that works. My eyes dashed around the room and everyone was staring at me, mom blocked my window.

I scrolled through a few pictures of dogs and people partying. There was a picture of private parts, girl private parts! I wanted to throw up. The parts weren't mine for reasons I was sure of. I kept scrolling and there were many more pictures, my head spun and I couldn't believe there were more than two pictures. Some details changed in the pictures that made a few of them obvious that they belonged to different people, I scrolled further in the gallery, and then my stomach almost lost it.

There "I" was, I started crying and mom took the phone. In the picture you could see my pink undies with my skirt hiked up a bit but stopped with the black strap that kept me prisoner in that stretcher. I could see a bit of my purple flannel shirt. I started to shake and Detective Williams asked me to take one more look and if I was absolutely certain that it was of me. Mom also looked at the exposed picture and she grabbed for the bag of belongings from the corner and showed the officer some of the clothes from within.

I felt sick, how many people had seen this picture? Why did he have to expose me and take a picture when he should have been helping me? What kind of sick disgusting freak would do such a thing? My stomach was heaving but I kept fighting to swallow it all back. I remembered Katie and how pretty and funny she was. I cleared my throat really hard and asked for the phone back. I didn't want to see any more lady parts but I wanted to make sure there weren't any more of me.

I scrolled deeper into the gallery and there it was, another picture of my private area, pink undies pulled to the side to see what they normally should have covered, mom dropped her head and said *"that explains the blood smear that I saw in that area"* mom uttered as she started to weep, I wanted to cry also but there was a rage, a confusion, a turmoil that flared in my chest that suddenly shoved my food back down into my stomach. There ended up being about four pictures that were revealing and very personal. There were other pictures in the gallery of different parts of women, some looked like they had been sent to him and I've heard of such things.

Anyone that would send these types of pictures are low class and now any girls that sent some of these pictures are now going to be opened up to judgment and ridicule from others and who knows how many people will be looking at such delicate photos. My head started spinning again and I tried not to think about how many people may see the most intimate parts of me. "Oh my god" is all I could mutter, Ms. Rollins stayed locked on my face while the officer was so very respectful and stared out the window.

I fought the urge for my eyes to roll back into my head but I did have to lay my head down for a few minutes. *"What next"* I asked the officer as he stood there rigid and stern. He asked me to positively identify which pictures of me were of "me" for certain and he turned the phone off without even needing to look at the pictures, which made me feel a little better. I didn't want my "private areas" waved all over half the earth; I'm not from jersey shore. The officer said there are a few people now that will have to catalog the pictures, find some information on them such as date, time, and origin then the prosecuting attorney will get involved.

Walker would be subpoenaed to not leave town and would probably face a form of work suspension now that there were some grounds for possible termination and legal punishment. I felt ill again, what if he had a family or something and he got in a lot of trouble? Is this all my fault? I felt terrible. Ms. Rollins spoke up and told me that she would talk with me some more in a few minutes. Mom kissed me on the forehead and followed Rollins and Williams out of the room.

My head spun and not even in the same direction as my stomach. My shoulders wanted to heave but I stared out the window as hard as I could. The sun was shining and my eye lids tried so hard to close. I felt sick and mad and my anxiety was going crazy, bouncing between my chest and my head and it all bottlenecked in my throat. My mouth was dry and it was difficult to swallow.

Mom and Ms. Rollins came back in; mom sat in the chair while Ms. Rollins took up a seat on the stool that sat under the sink. Both ladies sat by me and took turns speaking. Mom told me that everything was going to be ok and Ms. Rollins asked me what I was thinking about. My head spun in millions of directions and I didn't know where to begin. Mom saw the pictures as I did and she said they were just peeks at my private area but that I need to not think about it. Was she kidding? Someone violated me, I was so glad that someone was there to help me and then they used the opportunity to prey on me as I hurt just lying there.

I still felt ill, warm and began to sweat. Mom brushed my hair with her hands and encouraged me to listen to Ms. Rollins. Rollins explained that it wasn't just a snap of the fingers to make all of this go away and that there is a good possibility that I might have to testify in court. My jaw just dropped; will there be big pictures of my exposed little lady for a whole courtroom to stare at? A whole jury of people looking at my beat up body, and then staring back at "me"? Ugh I felt sick again.

Ms. Rollins ensured me that it is a discrete process and that the least amount of people necessary will have to see my intimate parts and that it is respectfully handled. She wasn't comforting me at all. She continued to speak and tell me that I have to be strong to make sure that this animal goes away and stops his vicious ways. WBC preyed on innocent people and got away with it by being in a trusting position, and had abused it.

Her words touched on my anger more than my fear and I felt a tad better. I shook and mom squeezed my hand tighter. My adrenaline was running top notch. I hated so many things right now. I hated this hospital, a man I had never seen, myself for not being able to stop what was happening to me, everything. I had so many feelings rushing over me and all I could do was let go and cry. I hated crying again.

Ms. Rollins and mom spoke for a bit and I couldn't hear through the weeping, then she left. Mom sat with me for a long time, I just cried until the sky turned a vibrant orange with light tufts of clouds sprinkled in the background. Mom told me that dad and Sara didn't know and would not know until I was ready to tell them. I didn't want anyone to know, I was so ashamed. How could any of this happen? How did I not feel my panties tugged and pulled like that? What happened to my leggings? Were they removed so he could do what he did or snagged when I was being pulled from the accident and he just took advantage of the opportunity?

I sat with mom and talked about Katie, I didn't want to talk about me anymore. We joked about her goofy antics, her bright smile, so many of the fun times we had had and won't ever have again. I missed her so much, mom did too. Mom reached into my book bag and pulled out the book that Mr. Matt had given me from Katie's collection. Mom suggested I read it and see if there was any solace within its pages. The book looked like it had been read a few times and I just imagined Katie sitting up in her room escaping to the farm inside its pages.

Mom helped me through dinner and made sure I was ok for her to leave for the night. I didn't want be alone after the day I had but I was super tired and it had been a long day for her too. I reassured her I'd be ok and then she left. Naiya came in to see how my day was and right away she knew it was a bad day. She sat quietly and told me to remember the strength of the little boy in her story and to be brave myself.

I told her about what all happened and the pictures and the officer. She kept her mouth closed but her eyes opened widely as I spoke. Naiya had disbelief in her expression and sadness in her forehead. Naiya left briefly to check on her few other patients but returned in a few minutes. Naiya let me just talk and work out my feelings about everything. Naiya helped me drink down a bunch of ice water and that helped to settle my stomach but my nerves were still pulsing through me. My body felt beat up again. I was tired and sore from therapy but my mind wandered too much for it to try to sleep anytime soon.

Naiya told me stories of her friends in California, spending time at the beach and her time here in nursing school. I liked listening to her as she spoke so eloquently. Speaking with her comforted me and it was a short relief in my day. Naiya was really sweet trying to distract me from the rigors of my day. My mind kept wandering, racing back and forth between the ambulance, the accident and the long road that I have traveled while recovering. I missed my home.

The night dragged on, every time I closed my eyes I was suddenly strapped into the stretcher, being uncovered and touched. I jolted awake on and off throughout the night, each time in a panic and a daze until I was able to regain my awareness of my surroundings. My head spun and was heavier each time I woke up. The room was dark and the shadows played tricks on my mind, I really didn't want to be alone, I pressed my nurses' button and it prompted Naiya to come in.

Naiya came and sat with me for a bit. I asked her to tell me more stories about the beaches in California and her life back home. Naiya smiled but looked weary as she began to speak. She told me stories of her and her friends going out on weekends to different beaches, all the sun tanned bodies packed together for their places on the sand, the radios blaring with the latest bumping beats, people dancing and playing Frisbee. Naiya said she enjoyed some of the beaches of Lake Michigan but nothing compared to back home.

Naiya continued to tell me stories of her and her girlfriends getting dressed in their cutest outfits to go to clubs and laughed at most of the wannabe's trying to dance, all the while they just chatted and carried on. She told me about many midnight runs to the beach and just running in the waves, strappy shoes in hand until the sun crested over the horizon behind them. I felt my eyes get heavy as I thought about frolicking in the warm water, sand sticking to my feet and toes. I pictured myself with Sara and Katie as Naiya narrated what we did in my drowsy stupor.

I slumped into sleep and this time it was more peaceful. I awoke Wednesday morning still feeling groggy from the crappy night of sleep but the sun was bright and my tree tops were swaying quickly. I keep imagining myself outside, at the park or walking around the neighborhood. I still couldn't shake the idea of being touched by a total stranger, I didn't like it and it sent chills through me each time I thought about it. I don't remember being touched but the visions still popped into my head. I felt sick all over again.

I picked through breakfast, my right arm hurt but I could remove it from the sling and work my fingers enough to hold a fork to cut my waffles.

Eating just made me feel more nauseous. I opened my laptop for a brief moment then decided just to close it and text Sara. She was also finishing breakfast, I wonder if all hospitals timed their meals? Sara asked me how I was holding up and let me know she was up for some bandage changes today. I wanted to tell Sara but I also didn't want anyone to know. I was ashamed and didn't want the pity.

I beat around the bush and hesitated talking much. I knew if I told her we would both cry and I was sick of crying. I had anger in my veins. I felt the surge pounding in my chest and my head was dizzying because of it. I was tired of feeling like a helpless little girl. I manned up and told Sara about the conference with mom, the officer and Ms. Rollins. Sara had a short response of "OH yeah?" she left the opening for me to continue. I felt the lump in my throat join with the pit in my stomach but I swallowed really hard and kept texting.

I told her about scrolling through all the pictures, the breasts, the "other parts" and the pictures Walker had of himself hanging out or drinking with friends. He seemed so normal and that it was hard to picture him as a monster. Sara was astounded that I had to look at so many pictures on his phone. I told her it was the same ragged phone I remembered seeing in the ambulance. I told her that mom had suspect about a blood spot on my undies and it was probably from him pulling them aside to peek at my downstairs. I wanted to cross my legs and lay lady like but this tube in my parts and my splinted legs made it impossible.

I felt hot, sweaty, and uncomfortable in my own skin but remembered the little boy from Naiya's story and swallowed hard; I wanted to cry again but fought it. I was tired of crying. I kept texting Sara and telling her about my nightmares, about what Ms. Rollins had spoken about, the officer and his mighty mustache and his rigid look. Sara urged me to keep telling her what I was thinking. I was shaking and it made my texting look horrible, but I pushed through it. I told Sara that I wondered how many of the other lady parts I had seen were of girls just wanting his help while he helped himself instead. I wondered if my private pictures were put online or shared and how many guys didn't know I was only fourteen?

Sara told me I can't think like that, my anxiety was already at its peak and my hands were shaking. My heart pounded as I kept telling Sara how scared I was for whatever lies ahead. Sara reassured me that she would do what she could and that mom and dad were right by my side. A text from mom popped up asking how I was today. I responded with "just hanging around" and she told me that she would call me in an hour. I wondered what else was going to happen. I wondered when I was actually going home.

Sara was jealous that I was headed down a path that would lead me home sooner than she was. I wasn't sure when I was going but just the rumor of leaving was enough to elate me. Sara told me she was to remain a guest in her hospital for at least two more weeks and there wasn't enough of a sign of leaving. I felt bad that she was trapped that much longer, I imagined she was just as ready to leave as I was, and just as ready to run too.

I texted back and forth with Sara for most of the morning, I sent a message to Bobbi asking for the latest homework assignments and thanking her for her help. Bobbi responded "that's what friends are for bestie" I appreciated her help and missed hanging out with her. She apologized that she hadn't been able to come see me, track was back on for the season and her parents were too busy with work and her brothers to run her out. She said she asked my mom to bring her out and that mom said she would when things lined up better. I understood, I was over an hour away and by the time track was out it was almost five and her parents had their hands full.

I missed Bobbi, I missed hanging out and having giggling girl time. My backside is sore again and trying to roll to adjust a pressure relief is tough. I am more and more tempted to remove my splints and move my legs, I had the splints off for therapy and I know I can put weight on them but I end up so sore afterwards. I asked Bobbi how she was able to text me so early, she told me that they were showing a movie in geography, "the distribution of population" she sounded so thrilled and yet, I actually missed sitting there with her.

Bobbi told me that track was as it always was, the preppy girls talking about nail polish and comparing their matching high ponytails while the boys ogled the eighth grade girls that were starting to develop. Those developed girls would parade a little longer in their sports bras in a "look at me" fashion in the locker room while complaining about the skeezey boys that they caught staring anyways.

I don't understand those girls, they hike their shorts up a bit higher to attract attention but complain when it's not attention from the one or two boys they want it from. These are the same girls that will strip down to their sports bra's when it gets barely warm enough and spend their time stretching and shoving their boobs in the air while staring at a few of the boys they deem worthy of their admiration.

There is always that one boy, Mike Ervin, a total scum bag, it's the history of man to acquire younger girls but this total loser scams on sixth grade girls like they have something to offer. He just tries to get kissed as often as he can under the excuse that he is an eighth grader but he is so nasty ugly that he looks like he might as well be from jersey or something.

He always has a stern ugly look about him, a giant under bite and pointy nose; he looks like Beavis that had bitten a lemon. He always had bad body odor problems; I know I don't smell like roses sitting here but shower man.

Mom called and interrupted my texting session. I answered and sounded mousy as I tried really hard to speak. My nerves were still unraveling and my head felt heavy as she spoke. Mom asked how I was coming along with my homework and it felt like small talk. Mom was always transparent when she had bigger things on her mind. Moms interlude lead to officer Williams, he called her this morning and informed her that Walker had been arrested and that there was a trial coming up, and that I would have to be there, I couldn't breathe.

chapter 15

MOM AND I hung up and I laid back dizzy and feeling sick. I told Bobbi and Sara that I would talk to them later as I wanted to be sick. I just turned my attention to my tree tops and tried to put all of this mess out of my mind. The day came and went as so many others have. I racked up text messages from people and parents but I didn't have the mental capacity to respond. Mark waltzed in and out while I put out a strong vibe that I wasn't in a talking mood. I picked at lunch and then dinner and let the day wind down.

Thursday started out restless and weary. I once again missed a good night's sleep but didn't have that busy of a schedule ahead of me anyways. Mark brought breakfast and tended to his tasks and ensured my comfort before he left. I watched the trees and texted back and forth with Sara for a bit. Today was a big day; Sara was being moved to another room on another floor, a sort of step down unit. Mom was with Sara for the move and checked in with me. I was glad Sara was slowly making progress, as was she.

Sara was still jealous that I was on my way home much sooner than she was. I was excited that I got to head to therapy today. John and Jose were two very cool and very funny guys and I was glad that I got to spend time with them. I did better at eating breakfast and tried rubbing my legs a bit to prep them for the exercise I was in for. Sara said her new room had a view of a forest and could see cars in the distance, much better than the side of the adjacent building, I can understand that; I laughed to myself.

A transporter came to get me for therapy about mid-morning; my phone last said ten just before I left my room. I rolled on down to the physical therapy ward and once again Jose was there to greet me. I was unwrapped from my leg splints and took up position in a wheel chair to make it to the walking rails again. I was nervous and my legs seemed to preemptively ache, they knew what was in store for them. John stood behind me to help me up and brace myself.

John and Jose seemed less uppity today, kind of somber as they worked and less than themselves in their usual harassment. They told me that this was our last session and that they'd miss me. I wasn't scheduled with them next week so that means I should be out of this hospital before next Tuesday. I took to my position holding on the rails and working on my stride as I walked back and forth down the ten foot handrails. My thighs were sore but it seemed to get a little easier walking.

John and Jose not being themselves bothered me, I looked forward to this for two days and now they are going to stiff me? I thought about what mom said, being strong for my older sister and having the strength to lead the way to recovery for her. I leaned for a moment against the rail as my right arm hurt from holding on. Jose spoke up *"take his hands boss"* as he smiled and nodded to John, then corrected himself and told John that he had to say it, just like in Green Mile, John laughed a little, I laughed a lot.

Jose shot a few more jabs at John while his defenses were down, John called a truce and they got back to work. After about twenty minutes of walking I was set on a machine called a NuStep and I half bike rode with a side of power walking I guess you'd say. The machine was awkward and I once again had to lie back on my sore tail bone. The workout was different and it felt good to get a good stretch to my legs but it was also tough. Other workers tended to other patients and John mostly coordinated with other workers while Jose stayed by my side.

My legs were sore after about ten minutes on the machine, my right arm also hurt. My mind changed tracks and started thinking about Walker and him touching me. Time seemed to slow as I trudged on while my arms pumped and my legs cycled. I thought about all the time I had spent on my butt, in pain, the surgeries, and having my pride attacked. I felt the rage fire up in my chest and I pushed harder on the machine while seemed to push right back. I felt my adrenaline rush through me, my veins felt on fire and it all throbbed in my temples. My jaw clenched tightly as I pushed through all the fear of getting hurt and through the pain of being hurt, I worked for the inner strength I needed to know I had.

I slowed my pace and as I slowed down I realized Jose had been talking to me, I felt bad that I had completely been ignoring him but I honestly didn't even hear him when he was trying to get my attention, I was focused. I felt my heart pounding but in a good way, I was perspiring and breathing hard and Jose coached me to keep rowing but to keep slowing down before coming to an abrupt stop. Jose helped me up and into a wheel chair and pushed me towards the tub again. I liked the tub as it was hot and relaxing, it smelled kinda funny but I didn't care. Helping me to keep everything about me, I stepped down to my waist and kept on moving my legs in and out to relax the muscles.

John joined us and he and Jose spoke about lunch ideas. They were talking pizza but couldn't agree on anywhere. They finally agreed on Q's pizza, not some nut job owned chain and shook on it, John excused himself to go order and Jose took a seat on the floor next to me but facing the opposite direction. He seemed sincere at his job, he did it well and he seemed to enjoy what he did. Jose told me that he and John he where both Navy men and vets at that. John Served during the Persian Gulf War and he during this latest mess in the Middle East, "the litter box" he called it.

Jose told me that he was born in Mexico and at a very young age his momma brought him here with her. He said that by joining the navy he got his citizenship and was able to serve a country he felt was his home his entire life. I was surprised Jose was telling me this, he told me that he and John joke because they both liked seeing patients feel better and watching them heal. Patients come and go and if you share too much you get attached and then they're gone. They were also very good work friends and have worked together splendidly for years, doing what they enjoyed.

Jose was sharing this information because he remembered me asking and that this was my last session with them. I felt sad and knew that I would miss them, which was crazy because I've only had half a dozen workouts with them and I've only been here a month or so. John had kids that were in college and he missed them, Jose continued to talk to me, "*he misses his kids and most of our patients are towards the end of their physical abilities so when the younger patients come to see us, they reminds him of his kids, that's also why he and I joke the way we do, I remind him of his son who is still enlisted*" I felt my eyes want to tear up a bit and thought about how hard it would be for mom and dad to watch their daughter head off to college, a bitter sweet moment but also a point in life that most people get to.

I was quickly overcome with the glad relief that neither mom nor dad had to bury one of us but then the joy also quickly melted to sadness as I recalled Mr. Matt having to have buried Katie. I was sad again. I wonder how he was doing. I wonder if seeing Sara or I in the neighborhood would remind him in a good way or a bad way about Katie. I wonder if his memories would be a tortuous reminder or a nice revisit of those memories. I sat in the big metal can and just thought. John appeared over my shoulder and asked what we were talking about, "oh my gosh" I quickly thought as I realized Jose was talking again and I completely phased him out and ignored him; *AGAIN*. Jose blurted out to John *"Hold on Jamie, you ain't no Fox!"* then chuckled.

I was up and out of the tub and once again, changing out of my soaked red gown and into my big baggy blue one. It felt really good to be free and unclad for a moment. I knew the room was private and while un-wrapped from the splints I felt relieved. I could see the scars on my knee healing, the little holes on my thighs healing over but still looking like little pink dimples and the scar on my arm raised and feeling kinda gross. My frail body looked a little better; my legs have mostly come back down to their original size compared to a few weeks ago.

I was kind of pale and could use some time outside. My stomach scar wasn't pretty and I was going to have to deal with it if I was ever going to wear a two piece bathing suit in public ever again. My hip bones jut out and I looked thinner than I was used to. Maybe I should have eaten a bit more as recommended by mom and Mark.

I was only unclothed for a moment and normally I'm very shy about my body, even when I'm alone but I realized that this little machine has pushed through so much and I've had more people look at parts of me than I ever could have wanted in my life, but here I am, I'm ok, healing and get-ting stronger. I've had wonderful help from John and Jose and with a great staff of nurses I'm progressing out of here soon. I quickly redressed into the dull blue gown with dark blue flower looking designs on it. I would almost prefer the red gown because it didn't feel as awkward or like it was falling off of me.

John knocked and we rolled over to the massage table for the last time. I felt uncomfortable with the muscle rub down still but there was a part of me that would also miss the attention. Jose and John rubbed down my legs and they pushed a bit harder on my thighs but it was a good pain. John reminded me that on my own I need to take it easy and not rush to walking or running so I can still heal. Jose left for a minute while John helped me to sit up. John said he was glad to have met me and appreciated getting to watch me heal.

John said he was proud of me for how strong I showed to be and even with pain staring at me I still followed directions and did the work. I was feeling stronger and I had a stronger perspective of myself. John said he had some bands for me to continue to work with. Jose came back in with some long blue rubber bands, they were cool, stretchy and Jose snapped John with one and said to be careful with them.

John showed me a few quick pulls that will help to strengthen my arm and that I can also use them to work on my legs as I sit and rebuild my muscles also. John and Jose helped me to make it back to my wheel chair and to stay covered discretely. I thanked them both and actually ended up hugging them both. I was thankful for my time with them as they were very funny. I climbed back onto my bed and glanced around the room for the last time before John pushed me into the hallway for the patient transporter.

We strolled on our walk back to my room, I laid back and stared at the objects passing overhead on the ceiling and tried to avoid eye contact with people staring at the girl wheeling by. It was uncomfortable and it once again made me insecure. I made it back to my room and the muscles in my legs still felt thick and throbbed a bit, my skin was cooling down after the tub and I shivered a bit because I was cold. Mark came in to make sure I was reattached to my monitor.

I ate lunch and knew it was a matter of time before Ms. Rollins came in for our Thursday meeting. I texted Sara to see how she was handling her new accommodations, she replied that she liked them so much better but was still getting used to her new nurses. I asked her how well she was looking forward to her physical therapy and she said that she really wasn't. I explained that even though it wasn't hopscotch it wasn't boot camp either. Sara and I didn't have much to chat about that didn't remind us of Katie, she was such a big part of our lives and in every way involved that there wasn't a topic that didn't lead back to us talking about her. I flipped open 3rd Hand Ranch and thumbed through more of the pages for a bit.

I found myself attaching to the one little blonde character, she had an inner trouble that was a large part of who she was as a character and like her, I knew that it was something that could be a great source of strength but happened to be a burden that was also too much too handle. I felt like what happened to me shouldn't have, I still felt like a victim of some perverse freak and that I was ashamed about something that wasn't my fault. I got teary as I read.

The book was hooking me and it was all I wanted to read but Ms. Rollins knocked on the door and let herself in. She greeted me for the afternoon and asked how I had been. I told her I was fine but she then prodded into my thoughts and feelings about Tuesday's ambush. My phone alerted with a text message but I didn't break eye contact with Rollins. I spoke about being nervous about what lies ahead of me and wondered what is going to happen to Walker. I felt bad that he was sitting in jail and it was my fault. Rollins' told me not to feel responsible for him getting in trouble for something *HE* had done.

Walker took advantage of an opportunity to use his position as a caretaker to sneak a peek at my private parts and then also to take incriminating photos that got him caught. I told her that there were several other photos of other girls' parts and things but that some of them looked consensual and maybe I was wrong. She encouraged me to tell her how I was certain which pics were of me, well I'd recognize my own body, come on.

I told her I recognized my skirt that was hiked up and also my pink panties that were tugged out of the way to expose "me". My head started feeling heavy and my anxiety started to flare up as I remembered the pics of my parts on that beaten up phone. I told her I was scared of how many people had seen the pictures and wondered how many people this jerk had sent them to. I told her I was scared that if I had to go to court everyone would be picturing my downstairs and asking me questions that would make me want to die, I was so embarrassed.

Ms. Rollins explained to me that there wasn't much difference in lady parts and that even though mine was mine, it wasn't something to get hung up on. Her words seemed like empty comfort words and I was still feeling sick about the ordeal. What if I had to look at the pictures on the phone in a full courtroom and then some jazzed up lawyer showed them around the courtroom to everyone and yelled out that I had identified my "lady parts" on that phone?

Rollins told me that court issues like this are smaller and discrete, I asked her how so, and she then described a scenario for me. She told me that usually in instances like these there is a woman judge and a few specific people that need to verify that the pictures were taken with the phone. Walker would be there through the whole thing and everyone would take this seriously. I still felt sick about people seeing my delicate parts; unwarranted and uninvited.

I closed my eyes and pictured a room full of people, everyone talking and whispering and staring at me. I didn't want the attention, I didn't want to focus, and I really didn't want Walker to stare at me and imagine my parts or relive what he had done. I wanted all of this to go away. My chest was tight and it was hard to breathe. Rollins told me that she would be there if I wanted her to be and that Williams had asked her to consider being a witness. I asked Rollins how she felt about everything and how much practice she had in situations like this.

Rollins told me that if I would consider letting her peek under my gown that she could also count as a medical validation regarding the pictures but there was no way I was doing that, I've had enough people look at my little lady. Mark came in and refilled my IV bag and gave me a nice few minute interruption with great timing. I was usually semi comfortable with Ms. Rollins but it almost felt like the short redheaded lady was out to look at my private parts the whole time. Was she really on my side or was she conning me the whole time? I felt trapped, betrayed, and very uneasy.

I clinched my legs together and tried to close myself off a little towards her. She kept talking about trial stuff and that it won't be easy for me but that I also needed to remember that without my testimony that he might not end up in trouble for what he had done. I remembered that Mike Ervin schmuck and how much I wished his spoiled self was tossed out into traffic for his neurotic behavior and thought about maybe he and Walker would someday share a jail cell, they could be boyfriends and Mike would probably like that. W.B.C. was in a position of trust and used it to the disadvantage of innocent people for personal gains of some sick freak that will end up in a caged hell.

My body was getting sore from my workout and my stomach was growling like crazy. Rollins talked on and on and I did my best to listen, I just wanted to stare out the window and watch the trees dance. I tried to keep my mind out of going to court, dealing with tons of people, and the circus that I remembered all TV court things being. My anxiety was running at top speed as I pictured a judge sitting high up on a bench, glaring at me, comparing cell phone pictures of my private parts and my little self, sitting across the room. Am I going to be the headline reason for the court thing?

Newspapers talking about some accident surviving little girl turned pedophile victim. What if his parents are there and shouting or spitting at me for accusing their son of this monstrous crimes. Can I look at the people that made WBC, such a hateful thing? Such an evil doing "man" that tries to do badly at any opportunity. I felt sick and I hoped that my time with her was over soon. I found it easier to use his initials because using his name just made me feel like I was strapped into that stretcher in the back of the ambulance, victimized all over again.

Ms. Rollins noticed that our time was up and she bid me farewell, she left me a business card with her name and work info on it if I needed to ever chat or get help with the court stuff coming up. I got to texting Sara and told her about what happened, she doesn't blame me for feeling strange and she said she felt weird about the Rollins conversation also. Sara said that I shouldn't worry much about what was ahead because the future only comes one day at a time, a line she read on some internet site I suppose. I still felt sick but hungry at the same time.

I text mom and asked her if she was planning on coming to see me that night at all, she wasn't but could if I needed her to make the hour drive from home, I didn't know what I wanted. Bobbi text in and told me the latest list of homework and apologized that track ran long so, that's why I didn't hear from her till now. I told mom I was fine and just feeling lonely and tired. Mom told me to hang in there and that I'd be home soon. I smiled lightly thinking about being home soon, no more chats about what happened, freedom from having to relive that nightmare night over and over, my room, my bed, my life back.

I wanted to be strong and courageous but I was still so scared of so much. I wish I knew what was going to happen. Sara text me and told me that courage was having the balls to do something no matter how scared I was, I guess that makes sense but it wasn't that comforting right now. Sara was right and I even told her, she told me that my being strong and taking on my therapy like a champ gave her courage to do it also and to not be afraid to do the work even at the deterrent of pain.

Amber came in and told me that she'd be my night nurse, she asked how I had been and I just shrugged, I was tired and even though I was starving, I hardly ate my dinner. Amber told me that she would stay and chat if I wanted her to but I just didn't feel like talking. It was getting dark out and I just wanted to lie back and watch the sky turn to a deep orange with purple swirls in it. The sky was vibrant and warm. I wanted to be outside, sitting on a lounge chair out back, the summer bug-zapper buzzing with random sparks of electrocuted critters in the background. My lounge chair was my silent, lonely place of peace at home, huddled up in a hoodie watching the sunset or reading, or doing both.

I let the night creep in; the darkness of the room grew, overtaking the room. I sat and waited for slumber to consume me. My body twitched and faded numbly as I felt myself drift to sleep. I kept my lounge chair and the orange hues of the sky in my mind. I kept thinking of that bug-zapper and tried to coerce my dreams to follow my thoughts that I had focused on.

chapter 16

FRIDAY MORNING WAS nothing different than so many others. Mika and Tyson came in for a final check on my legs. I was unwrapped and both residents looked over my legs, bent and straighten my right leg, Tyson put his fingers on my kneecap as I flexed my leg. They told me that I was free of the splints and no longer needed the itchy wrappings. I was told that I would have a leg brace for my right leg to wear over the next two weeks and to limit my walking to less than half an hour at a time for the first week and an hour each time the following week.

I felt my excitement come up at the thought of going home. Mark came in with a big black brace, it looked like a giant bunch of Velcro and gears, and it was rather scary. Mark said that once we got the brace strapped on that I would be losing a lot of my tubes also. I smiled pretty big at the thought of being untied from machines and beeping contraptions. I asked him how much different I would feel without some of the IV's. He warned me that I would feel more pain as they have been stepping me down from the pain meds but I would have pain meds avail when I needed them.

Mark removed my IV tubes from my arm, it hurt for a second and was kind of gross watching the plastic needle slide out of my skin. He stuck a small Band-Aid over the hole with a cotton ball pressed against it. Mark removed the blue pump thingy that was on a wheelie pole and then returned. Mark looked at me for a moment and said there was one more tube that he had to remove, I gave him a serious look and then I remembered that he was talking about the tube that was jutting out of me in the bad place.

Mark asked me to lay back and he would be quick and gentle to remove my catheter. He asked me to take a deep breath and to breathe it all out and relax my muscles "down there". I was nervous for a moment, I felt a pressure release inside of me as I heard a whisping sound real quick. He counted from three to one and on one he removed the hose that was inside of me, I clinched my eyes but also peeked to see him remove the hose that fed into my girly parts slide out from under my gown.

I felt a small tingle as it slid out of me and he pushed a piece of gauze against me for a moment, I didn't want to be touched but that was the last thing that had me tethered to anything, I felt free. The tube was a lot bigger than I expected it to be, I couldn't imagine that it fit in my tiny body but it certainly felt a lot larger than it looked, it felt like a turkey baster! Mark let me know that I would be here all day but that probably midday Saturday would be my official parole hearing. I smiled at his joke, especially because he knew I kinda felt like a prisoner here.

My delicate parts felt a little swollen and not right down there but without that tube dangling out of me I felt as though I was getting back to normal "down there". Mark told me that I had to leave the sticky patches on my chest for the remainder of the night so they can monitor my heart beat as I'm no longer on IV pain meds. I felt totally different now lying in bed, I was totally free except for the brace on my right leg and my right arm still slung around me. I can't believe I've been here for a month. I wonder what I have missed at school.

Are the boys' still giant tools? Popped collars and fake tans, skinny jeans still looking like they pooped in their pants, thinking they are cool or that girls still liked that sort of thing? OK so maybe I'm not ready to go back to school but I'm ready for my comfy bed. I terribly miss my thick blankets, my TV, being able to come and go. My tree tops were swaying as lunch came in. I didn't do much today but my stomach was growling. The Philly cheese-steak was superb and my tiny body might have made enough room for a second one.

Mark brought crutches in for me to lean on so I didn't have to place all my weight on my right leg yet. Sara was very glad to hear that I was be-ing detached from everything. Sara wasn't enjoying her therapy and said is felt like another car accident. I couldn't blame her for feeling that way but she also said I handled it well and was jealous I was catheter free. I had the urge to pee, I was a little nervous because I've had the feeling to pee for weeks but haven't had to worry about it either. I wrangled my crutches and scooted to the left side of my bed to make this venture happen. I didn't like the feeling of the sheets and blankets of my bed rubbing against my butt as I scooted, I didn't like this backwards robe leaving my hind end dangling in the wind.

I slid down and onto the crutches; I stabbed them into my arm pits trying to keep my balance as I steadied myself on my legs and the crutches at the same time. I hobbled to the restroom and felt a bit of a relief when my butt finally touched the freezing cold seat beneath me. Not to talk about peeing but it burned pretty bad and it took a try or two to get things, "flowing". I sat there for a few minutes and managed to pull up on the crutch and lift myself on my left leg, once my straight right leg was under me I could better bear weight to get my hands washed and back to the safety of my bed.

I made it back to the bed and even though I was feeling sore, and VERY drafty, I smiled just realizing what I had just done by myself. I spun and managed to lie back down, gently dragging my encased right leg back to its position. Using my butt cheeks to scoot and slide I managed myself back into position. I shoved a pillow under my left side to ease the pressure on that spot that was sore at the top of my butt crack from laying on it so long.

It felt like a twenty minute exercise doing the work of going to the bathroom and back. I was finally comfortable and I had to boast a bit to Sara that I was able to pee on my own. No, bodily functions and fluids aren't a lady like topic but I did it on my own. I bragged about being able to stand and move semi freely but also warned her that things down there burned to pee. Parts of me still tingled a bit as I re-covered myself using my good left arm. I was tired from all the hassle and trouble but the sense of independence was well worth it. I liked that I was working towards my freedom.

The Band-Aid on my arm didn't stay long; I figured once I was done bleeding from the little hole the IV sat in all month, that skin tugging Band-Aid had to go. Things were surreal as I sat there. I continued to sit there and reflect on everything that had happened, this is one of those situations that makes the world seem enormous, and yet our little home town seems so small, kinda like coming back from a long road trip and that final drive home.

Sara and I spoke about how much longer she had left, how jealous she was that I was headed home the next day. We spoke about Katie and how we both wished that she was there, at home with us. My excitement was up and I kept smiling thinking about being at home, returning to my life, most of my family and back to my youth. It's only been a month but so much has happened. I had to loosen the brace on my leg because it was starting to throb a bit, felt sweaty, and my toes were freezing.

Sara said she was still sore all over, that tube they shoved into her rib cage had actually went between her ribs and it was sore to inhale, and she was still pretty bruised from it. She said the scar on the left side of her head was healing over but the shaved spot felt fuzzy and strange. Mom texted in and said she got a good phone call about the official discharge time, and that she and dad would be here to help me out.

I liked that mom and dad would both be here. This whole month felt like one of those situations that would change me from the carefree little girl that I used to be and into a lady that can do anything. I thought about relearning to walk, the surgeries, just everything. The glass screams didn't shriek so loudly in my head but once in a while I had one accompany that flash of headlights that ignited the whole thing. Mark came in and asked me how I was getting about, I told him about my struggle to the restroom and back. Mark told me that the bladder is a muscle and without having been used in a month, that it might take a few tries to get it back to doing its job on command.

Sara said she can't wait to have her catheter removed; it was awkward and still very uncomfortable for her. Mark told me that in time things will return to the way they were. Mark reminded me about my walking restrictions and to keep the crutches nearby, he also used a washcloth and some tape to pad the arm rests so they didn't beat up my armpits so badly, I thought it was a good idea. Mark headed out on his way again. I texted Bobbi and told her the good news, she later responded that she would text my mom and see if she could join them to see me.

Lunch came, I actually finished the whole thing this time, the turkey sandwich could have used some yellow mustard but nonetheless it was good. I wanted moms home cooking; I wanted chili. I text dad and told him that I was craving Mongolian BBQ and asked if we could make that happen next week. He told me that my wish was his command.

I watched the trees sway again, I have trees at home but they weren't these trees. These trees, I convinced myself, were especially for me. I wanted to be curled up in a blanket and a hoodie and just sit quietly in the lawn chair on the back deck. I was so restless and I wanted to leave; now. I wanted the fresh breath of cold air to fill my lungs, that crisp spring morning air that smells of budding leaves and the summer to come. I wanted to watch the seasons come and go, the leaves unfurl, blossom, change colors, wither and fall to the ground again, the cycle of biology that marks that progression of the years as we all hustle along with our lives hardly noticing most of the time.

I wonder what I'll be doing this time next year; will Sara and I grow and in time talk about Katie less and less? Will Katie become less and less of a thought? Will Mr. Matt and Ryann move on through their lives and will

Katie just become a distant memory? I vow to name my first born daughter after her, in her honor, in her memory. I miss her so much and I'm sure everyone else does too.

I wasn't ever sure I'd know what I wanted to do with my life. I didn't ever think I wanted to settle down to one career choice and limit myself to doing one thing in my life. Dad was an underwriter and mom a paralegal, both of them enjoyed what they did however mundane it seemed. I wanted more out of my job, the rewards of helping people and seeing my work in each person, not just papers on a desk. After all of this is over maybe the medical field is the way to go, maybe one day I'll see some young, scared, hurt girl come in, in need of help, and be the one to help her.

I've received great care from many of the individuals at this hospital. Maybe that's what a hospital is, many great, talented, caring people all working together to help each other, and complete strangers. I'm sure like many companies, the middle management and top heavy business side is the boot that stomps out a lot of the progress though. I read articles of big hospitals laying people off only to put large bonus checks in the pockets of people that run the place but money and power taints everyone I suppose.

It's a shame when you get into the business of something and forget about the people you are helping and focus more on numbers. Dad tells me that he gets to help young parents acquire homes to start families and mom smiles thinking about helping right wrongs in many of her cases. I really think I want to spend my life helping much like those around me. With good timing Mark came in again to check my pain and comfort levels, I was sore but doing ok.

I texted with Sara and Bobbi on and off through the rest of the afternoon, trying not to brag to Sara about almost being free, I felt bad and wished she could be also, she said she'd probably be out in two weeks or so. Bobbi was looking forward to seeing me this weekend, we decided to play scrabble and lay low while we could. I was sure I was behind on my homework and would get more next week. I wanted to do anything but think about the trial that was due any day.

Of course not thinking about the court stuff put it at the forefront of my mind. I started thinking about crutching in to a giant courthouse, people staring at me as I hobbled my way through. Sitting in the courtroom laying eyes on Walker for the first time and wondering what was on his mind. Was he regretting what he had done? Will he have the integrity to apologize and own his actions like a man or deny everything like a chicken coward? Nowadays no one seems to take responsibility for their actions;

the news is rife with scumbags, shootings and killings and then people fleeing like rats.

I don't understand what in life is worth throwing away the only life you have to risk spending it in jail. I couldn't imagine how it's cool to have to shower with a bunch of strange people; I often wondered how being in jail gives you "street credit" or how that makes you cool. I wonder so many things about people; how trends become just that and how people think stupid things are some strange way to make themselves cool. I think belly button rings are cute but you get these freak shows that tattoo or pierce their faces, really? What kind of job besides pumping gas would really hire these people? I wouldn't even go to a coffee house with someone like that working there, it's disgusting.

The court stuff kept taking over my thoughts intrusively, a room full of suits and professional looking people using big Latin words and shouting things like "I object", what does that even mean? My excitement slid into anxiety at these thoughts of court and all the stuff involved, I was getting nervous again. I text mom and I told her I was nervous, she said that court was pretty simple and that everything would be ok. I trusted her but it didn't settle my nerves at all. I laid back and wiggled my toes and feet for a bit, they felt cold and laying here for as long as I have, it was something, about all I could do to pass the time.

I kept watching out the window between texting sessions with Bobbi and Sara. The day grew bright then began to fade as the afternoon passed on; I was so super thrilled that my time to leave was drawing closer. I don't think I'll be able to sleep tonight. Mom said she and dad were getting the house ready and that this past month has left it a mess in the midst of the chaos. Dad spent a lot of time in the garage with Mr. Matt because guys can bond and talk in a garage, I guess that makes sense. Mom had been busy spending most of her free time between the two hospitals so cleaning and such has fallen behind.

My parents worked hard at their jobs and we girls tried our best to help out. Mom usually did a lot of the running between track and cross country meets Dad usually came home late as he had a longer drive than mom. I felt bad that they both had to work so much. Mom worked part time when we were younger but a few years ago they told us mom was going back to work to help save for our colleges and that during the summers we were old enough to fend for ourselves. The summers were spent running and playing and we occasionally had trips or whole weeks spent with grandparents. The weekends were really nice when we could all spend family time together.

I started thinking about Katie again. I really hoped she was at peace when she passed. I hope that she was just asleep, having dreams of our fun times or some of her favorite memories. I flipped open the book that Mr. Matt gave me; I smiled thinking about the silly dog in the pages and also felt bad for each girl in it. I re-secured my pulse and calmed down a bit. As I read on I felt my blood pressure rise during the more intense parts and felt sad during others'. I really liked the book and looked forward to reading it on the back deck and finding out what each girl becomes.

I watched the sky grow dim, the reddish orange colors that slowly took over the blue of the afternoon, the changing of the light spectrum as the sun got farther from my single small spot on this giant world. The world was both big and small at the same time. We're no different than the ants we see in colonies all over the sidewalk, our sidewalk has a lot more to it but I know from the sky we are nothing more than small specks, insignificant blips on the time radar.

Pictures from space aren't that different than staring out into a field from a tall tree. Each person has their own interests, hobbies, likes and dislikes and we each strive for our own piece of property, to establish our own sense of self, and by doing so; it makes us all the same. If I had died my parent would have mourned, my friends cried, but life would have gone on, sand would have sifted through the hourglass of life and in a hundred years I wouldn't have even been a thought. It's sad that in our lives we interact and establish relationships but yet when we pass on that's it. A small spark in the billions of years the earth has been around.

Very few people make a big enough splash in the life ocean, very few names take up more than a page or two in history and every few generations that progress on, replace the ones before them. It's numbing that life is so fragile and that we are bundles of little cells, each cell performs a job, grows and dies and this happens millions of times a day and we aren't much different. Society has millions of people, also all performing a task, a job, a purpose, but at the end of a millennium, we are all forgotten while the rest of the societal body continues to live.

I'm sad at thinking of life as so meager, not pointless in any way but insignificant when you look at the whole picture. I guess I'm being philosophical because I was so close to having passed away and I want to find that greater purpose that I can serve. I want to be one of those names that make a whole page in history and someday some teacher might focus on, a person that thousands of other students might have to learn about. A girl becomes a lady; then possibly a legend. It seems like a huge task to go from a tiny girl and an even smaller speck in the world but somehow she morphs into a giant larger than life story, a legend maybe.

I hope that by journaling my endeavors that one day girls might read my pages, read my story, find the strength that I have struggled to find and the courage to do what is right and not back down. I am terrified of the next few weeks. Will kids at school only know me as the girl that was molested in an ambulance? Or as the girl that struggled to overcome a beaten and tattered body and still walk proudly into a courtroom, stare at her predator and hold her head up high?

I won't lie; I am scared out of my mind, worried that everything I have done will be forgotten, worried that I may be another statistic about abuse or just some picture that leaked online that other girls will just think to themselves "won't happen to me" or some ignorant comment. I want girls to know that doing the right thing isn't easy but it's why it's the right thing to do regardless. I want girls to think that they are worth more than anyone might think, we aren't just girls, and we make up a larger percentage of the population for a reason. We are daughters, sisters, and the only ones that can become mothers. We are life givers, not property!

chapter 17

SATURDAY MORNING CAME; I hardly remember falling asleep last night. I barely remember feeling so giddy upon waking besides Christmas mornings when I was younger. I felt older, like I had aged ten years in the past few weeks, Sara greeted me with a "good morning free bird" text and mom's text wasn't far behind. I smiled so much knowing that today was my parole date. I was a guest here for five weeks to the day and each day dragged on but each week seemed to fly by.

I felt strong but my leg was sore from the brace. I took it off to itch. Mom said she and dad were on the way shortly. Dad asked me if I had any requests that he could bring with them. I definitely wanted some junior mints and a red Gatorade; he said "not a problem". I didn't know what to do for the remaining few hours I had left. I was too full of energy to sit still and wait. The clock ticked by and I wanted to go now, ugh waiting sucks.

Naiya came in for the morning and informed me that she picked up the shift, I was glad to see her. She helped me pull the sticky patches of my chest and used an alcohol wipe to clean most of the sticky residue off of me. I still had square red marks all over my chest and torso and from above they kinda looked like an upside down smiley face. Naiya said that I should text my parents and ask them to bring me some sweats to wear home as the air was cold and the gown wasn't "styling". I sent that text real quick like.

Naiya sat with me for a few minutes here and there between call lights she had to attend to. I thanked her for all of the time she spent with me, keeping me company and sharing her inspiring words that helped me to find my own courage. Naiya said that everyone needs someone some times, other times people need the idea of someone that was stronger than them at a point to give them a strong sense of self. I thought about that on and off over the next few weeks.

As the morning dragged on I gathered what I could manage from my post in the bed. I wanted to save my strength to walk out of here. I put all of my belongings in my bag and got myself semi situated to wait. Naiya brought in lunch and let me know this was the last hospital meal I had coming. It was grilled cheese with steamed veggies. I picked out the cauliflower because that stuff is nasty and the rest just mushed down my throat. I ate with anticipation of mom and dad being here any minute. Each minute seemed to take hours and I tried to watch the tree tops but my eyes kept drifting to the door.

A knock hit the door, my heart beat raced and my pulse started pounding through my neck. Mom came in smiling, Dad was close on her heals and almost pushed her through the door. They both hugged me tightly and mom and I both cried. This was it, I was free!! Dad had misty eyes and told me that it was time to go home, HOME! Dad gathered my things and made his way to the car as mom helped me to get dressed.

I slid into fresh undies and mom looked at the little scars on my legs, pushing gently on each one. Mom then looked at the scar that ran down my thin right leg and she rubbed a bit on the red spots that were still there from the brace. I put that brace back on after we slid sweat pants on. Mom helped me into socks and I wrangled a t-shirt over my head followed by a hoodie. I looked like crap and I hated being all grungy wearing sweats out in public but oh well at this point. Dad came back with a wheel chair and Naiya by his side.

Naiya helped dad manage me into the wheel chair, I swung to the right as I sat up. Mom brushed my hair back and then helped me to stand up. I sat in the chair and felt the cold fabric chill my clothes. Mom grabbed my garment bag and tucked it under her arm. Dad pushed the chair and we slowly made it out into the hallway. Some of the nurses stood at the station and clapped, I hadn't met most of them but they cheered for me and my recovery just the same. I felt myself welling up with pride and some tears. I wished Mark had been there, I would have liked to thank him for his time and all that he had done to help take care of me. Naiya escorted us to the elevator, she stopped and smiled real big, I could see happiness in her eyes. I hugged her long and hard and thanked her so much again. Mom hugged her briefly as well.

We stepped out of the elevator and dad left me by the big windows near the door. Mom squatted down beside me as dad ran to get the car. Dad pulled the Fusion around and got out to open doors as mom lead me out. The air was brisk and chilly but was also warming and fresh. I took a few big breathes and even though reluctant to be leaving, knew that my time here was done. I hobbled into the car. Dad drove and mom sat in the middle of the back. I rode shot gun but with everything that happened I was a little uneasy. Mom just played with my hair and talked.

The whole ride home was without radio, mom and dad taking turns asking me millions of questions; like I had just gotten back from summer camp and they hadn't spoken to me for a month. My leg was a bit sore from having to remain straight but it felt good to actually have pants on. My undies gave me a bit of a wedgie but it was so much of better feeling than the catheter and the sheets on my skin.

We made it to the house where Bobbi was waiting for me in the house. Mom told me that she let Bobbi know that she was welcome in but that she and dad wanted family time coming to get me. Dad dropped my crap in the living room and I hobbled on my crutches in the door. My socks were wet from the pavement and I kicked them off once inside. Oh it felt so nice to have the carpet under my feet instead of the tile floor. The carpet felt great as I made feet fists with my toes. Mom told me to take care of what I needed to and that we were headed back out in ten minutes.

I told her that I wanted to see Sara really bad, she smiled and told me that it was already on the agenda. Bobbi was going to join us to head to Ann Arbor to see her. I was tired from all the excitement but also still amped up and wanting to see my sister. I texted Sara and let her know I was free and we were on our way. Sara said she would be happy to see us. Bobbi and mom took the back seat and I wedged myself into the front again. I turned best I could so I could talk to mom and Bobbi from the front.

Bobbi asked a bunch of the same questions that mom and dad did, things like "what it was like for me to sit there, what the surgery was like, how awful the catheter was?" I laughed and told her that having a hose hanging from me was like a fake penis but that I am glad it was temporary, dad just raised an eyebrow and chuckled at us girls and how silly we were. Bobbi and I did most of the talking with mom and dad having a few words in between. I missed her so much.

The drive took over an hour, Bobbi and I talked about classes, teachers. I spoke about John and Jose, making everyone in the car laugh retelling some of their quips and how they busted each other's' chops. Bobbi said that track was gearing up for meets in the next few weeks and like usual, most of the girls saw practice as social hour, the boys checked out the girls in their running shorts and the chestier girls flaunted what they could during stretches and such. It has only been five weeks but I was curious to see who changed and how.

Ann Arbor is a big busy town, stupid college kids walking all over the streets and stupid round about things in the roads. We pulled into a parking lot and made our way to see my sister. Finally up to her floor, I wasn't thrilled to be back in a hospital so soon but I crutched quickly to get to her room. Mom walked quickly next to dad to lead the way while Bobbi and I trailed behind. All the nurses wore navy blue scrubs and the nurse techs wore green. This floor resembled mine in so many ways yet it felt different.

Dad knocked on the door and we entered, Sara adjusted herself for visitors and smiled so big to see us. Sara had tears in her eyes and was so relieved to see me, as much as I was to see her. We hugged immediately and both cried a little bit. She cried out "I'm so sorry sis" I tried to tell her that it wasn't her fault but her tight hug and my crying made it hard to mutter the words. I sat on her bed and we hugged for a few minutes till both of our noses began to run. We both left each other's shoulders wet with tears. Everyone else just stood near the door until our embrace broke. I looked Sara up and down, she had a lot more leads running from under her gown to a monitor, her legs were puffy under her blankets, and her left arm was slung around her chest like my right arm was before.

Sara turned to me to give me a better look at the fuzzy patch that used to be long brunette hair on the left side of her head. Bobby said she could always rock the "G.I Jane look" and her eyes got real big in disgust at the suggestion. Mom and Dad asked her how she was holding up and they made some small talk. Sara said she was still pretty sore, talked about her physical therapy and that she didn't get a hot tub, just two non-petite women yanking her around for an hour each time. I felt bad that she was missing out on guys like John and Jose, making me glad I had them.

Bobbi looked uncomfortable but asked how her catheter was, Sara laughed and told her it was how she thought it would be, awkward but a decent relief from the constant up and down to pee, then Sara and I laughed at her odd curiosity. Sara jokingly offered to show her and everyone shuttered, shouting "NO" in unison and we all chuckled at her joke. Sara spoke more about her stay and her intense desire to be free of this place. I totally understood how she felt, like a prisoner without any chains or bars but also like a dog running to the end of its leash and only being able to bark.

We all hung out and talked till late afternoon. I didn't want to leave but I was getting hungry and Sara was getting tired from her day. We hugged more and said our goodbyes. We all made our way back to the car, instead of heading back to the highway we headed into town more. I didn't recognize our surroundings and my curiosity forced me to ask where we were going. Dad said he was fulfilling my request and that we were only a block from our destination. Ann Arbor was a mess of cars and screwy traffic patterns.

Dad found a parking spot and said "dinner is over there" with a head nod notion. I was starving and wanted to rid my body and taste buds of all that hospital food. This town seemed so big with all the tall buildings and people walking all over the place. I felt like a bum crutching around in sweatpants but as we turned the corner there it was, "Mongolian BBQ", the mecca of awesome food. Once inside, Bobbi and I compared how many foods we were going to load into our bowls and how much we were going to eat.

The place was crowded and busy, it was hard to get through all the people but dad helped me to get my bowl. I loaded up chicken and beef, tons of veggies, spiced it up with the amazing shitake mushroom sauce and headed to the grill. There were four guys at the grill, slicing and dicing and putting on a show for the lines of customers waiting to get their food cooked. There was a tall guy with crazy side burns running the show, he was loud and moved quickly all over the place.

There were all sorts of people filling the tables of this restaurant, so much commotion but the tall chef guy was at the center of most of the attention. There was a shorter stocky dirty blonde haired guy working as his number two. They slid out the food on the big grill and got to work with their big silver blades, cutting and chopping and twirling about. Food was scraped onto our plates and we snaked our way back to our table. We ate well and gulped down tons of the fantastic lemonades as the evening wound down.

We made the hour journey back home after all was said and done. I was super tired after such a long day but I was kind of scared to fall asleep only to wake up back in the hospital. We dropped Bobbi off at her house and the three of us headed home. Dad helped me out of the car and we were finally home for the night. I was relieved to be at home, I laid down on the couch for a bit and mom got to putting things away.

Dad tossed me the remote as he dug into his newspaper. I felt like a guy flipping channels the way I did. It was such a stupid thing but it was so nice having more than eight channels at my fingertips. Half an hour of mom and dad barraging me with questions and asking me what I needed and how I was doing later and I was ready for bed. Mom drew me a bath and oh it looked so nice. Pink soaps smelling so good and my giant pink fluffy towel on the rack, all waiting for me. I was home and loving it.

I soaked my body for a while in the tub; being in the water I instinc-
tively bent and straightened my legs like I was in the therapy tub again. The
bubbles covered me and I felt such a relief washing myself. I enjoyed shaving
my legs and getting all girlied up again, sitting in that hospital so long I felt
gross, almost mossy. Getting out of the tub was nerve racking as I tried to
carefully lift myself out and balance so I didn't put too much weight on my
bad leg and not risk slipping and wrecking myself standing on the good one.

In my pajamas and in bed, mom kissed me on the cheek and tucked
me in, she and dad were both very relieved to have me home and both bid
me goodnight. I laid there in my comfy bed, covered in the sheets that were
so much softer than those in the hospital, I felt weird finally being at home
but part of me missed the racket in the hall and my window with the trees
outside of it. I missed Naiya checking in on me and the other nurses that
kept eyes on me. I was thirsty and reached for my usual Styrofoam cup full
of water, that wasn't there.

I drifted to sleep with the lavender scented pillows that supported
my head. I tossed and turned all night, I was almost too comfortable, as
weird as it was. I woke up in the morning to mom cooking and dad thumb-
ing through another paper, how much news could he handle? That junk was
negative and tiring. I asked what was planned for the day and the only thing
they had planned for me was to lay low and relax. I was tired of lying around
and wanted some mental stimulation, I needed some action.

I got dressed in jeans and a shirt then text Bobbie to see if she could
come over. Mom pushed me to lay low and relax but I wanted out. Bobbi
rode her bike and I loaded up my custom crutches. We really didn't do
much but hobble around the neighborhood but it was so awesome to be
outside. We made our way to the park, I texted mom that I was ok and
that things were fine. Bobbi and I took up seats on the swings and watched
as kids played on the wooden structure

Kids ran around as Bobbi and I swung. It was nice to just swing
back and forth, talking about the hospital, the accident and the wreck. The
conversation lead to the ambulance and all that I remembered. Bobbi just
listened as I spoke and recalled what happened, the phone and the pictures
of the body parts on it. I told her how worried I was about the court stuff
coming up and wished it wasn't me. I wished so hard that none of this happened.

Bobbi told me that there was a school "dance" coming up and that
it would be great if we went together like usual to make fun of our fellow
classmates. I wanted to go just to be out of the house but also the idea of
the dance sounded funny and entertaining. I must have sat on those swings

for a while, the sun got warm and we had no need for the hoodies for the time being. We sat in silence for a little while; my mind wandered all over for a while as my feet made different designs in the woodchips. I was glad to be out of the hospital but didn't really want to go home either; out here my mind was kind of at ease and away from everything that was to come.

Bobbi and I headed back home a while later. I crutched slowly and Bobbi kept pace with me. I didn't really want to talk much more while Bobbi and I just moseyed along. I wondered what was going to happen to me, what was I going to do with my life? The future was so scary and had so many options in it. What if Walker thought about the same thing but ended up in his situation out of boredom or maybe he even just thought that it would be funny.

I really hope he didn't send anyone pictures of my parts, that is my delicate area and mine alone, and he violated that, and me. How would I tell future boyfriends or a potential husband? Would I be ashamed forever or be looked upon like a tramp because someone else saw my private area unsolicited? I feel so dirty that I was exposed like this. I know so many famous girls slutted up and put out sex tapes and have shown their private parts all over the internet but I want to be classy, tasteful and I have self-respect. All of this made my stomach sick.

Maybe I just lacked the sense of self that some of these girls had or the avenue to marketing that a naked girl brings. A real man should want to know the inner woman and not be in a hurry to see her naughty bits. Men lately have turned to pig brained morons that just want to lay with a girl and that's why if a real man respects you, he'll wait to get you undressed. I wish more people had the old school morals or even morals at all anymore, true gentlemen should want a lady, and a lady should be one to get herself a true gentleman.

If Walker had realized the trauma he could have caused by pulling his stunt on a young girl, the ramifications, the pain, he might have had some self-restraint. Maybe he was thinking that because I was in and out of consciousness that he could get away with it? Why would he think what he did was ok? Was he even thinking at all? He couldn't be such a moron could he? As an EMT isn't there a questionnaire or some form that would help them to figure out he was a sicko? I hated a man I didn't even know, I hated hating.

An intelligent person would see the outcome of their actions, the results that their actions could have. Respecting each other would make the biggest changes in the world possible if only people were smart enough to understand that. It's shameful to see when one person takes advantage over others or use easily manipulated people in such sick ways that WBC did. I felt an anger towards a man that I didn't know, I felt sick about everything.

I made it home that Sunday and spent the rest of the night just thinking, I wanted to shut my brain off and was worrying myself sick over everything. The night grew dark as I sat on the couch watching cars drive by. I missed watching the tree tops sway. Dad flipped channels before stopping on the history channel. I half watched some special on ancient boats and cultures, it further made me think about how insignificant we as people are, our lives spent running about and at the end of it all, wondering what we accomplished.

I laid down for my second night at home, no hospital, and no monitors beeping me to sleep. My eyes searched for dim lights on the other side of my closing eyelids. I felt the dark take over me and I just felt my body covered in my soft sheets. My luscious bed cradled my body and I rolled to be a bit more comfortable. I didn't really feel comfortable laying here nor really that tired.

I fell asleep after a long time laying there. My body was more tired than my mind. I was worn out and though it was a great relief to be home it was still foreign to be here. I spent five weeks longing to be home and it was still almost too good to be true. I missed having Sara in the room next door. I wished she was home and that in the morning we were heading to school together.

Monday morning came and mom stayed home to make sure I had hands if I needed them. Dad was off and gone before I roused out of bed. I showered and made myself up. Standing in the mirror I looked at myself before getting dressed, I still had the square pink marks on my chest from the sticky things for the leads. My hip bones still stuck out and my legs looked feeble. I didn't like the scars on my legs but I guessed there was nothing I could do about them. As I dressed for the day I slid my jeans over my beat up looking legs. I put on my tops and slid into another warm soft hoodie, meant to relax and still be able to do what I needed to. I left that steamy bathroom and made my way down stairs.

I laid down on the couch in the living room, mom came up from the basement doing laundry and made me breakfast. I felt bad that she was still kinda waiting on me hand and foot. Mom received a phone call and excused herself to the kitchen to take it. She spoke for a bit as I flipped channels trying to find something to interest me. Mom came back in and asked me to turn it off. She had a semi-serious look on her face and it put me on defense.

chapter 18

MOM CLEARED HER throat as she began to talk, my anxiety started to fire up. Mom told me that the phone call was Detective Williams and that he would like to see us. My head started to get dizzy, like I was about to get onto a big rollercoaster. I had a lump in my throat as I sat up. Mom helped me to my feet and I grabbed my crutches and then we headed off. I texted Sara about the latest events as we drove to the police department to keep her up to date; and to release some of my tension. It didn't take us long to arrive, there was a local state police department and it was the one mom went to originally when she contacted the detective a few weeks back when things seemed strange to her.

We parked and I needed a minute to get my head on straight, I was getting nervous and scared at the same time. We exited the car and I crutched my way to the big double glass doors. The parking lot was full of squad cars and trucks, officers were coming and going as well as many other people through those doors. Mom held the door open for me and a uniformed officer held the inner door; mom thanked him as she walked past, right behind me.

Detective Williams stood firmly behind the counter and greeted us good morning. The shorter officer lady behind the desk hit a button and Williams walked around a corner to let us in through another set of doors. Behind the big wood door was a hallway with lots of other doors. Williams led us into a conference looking room that had a huge dark wood table surrounded by big black chairs. The room was dull green in color, wood blinds and a large dry erase board on the far wall.

The lump in my throat grew and I was getting nervous being here, the walls seemed to close in on me. I crutched in and the detective pointed to a set of chairs for mom and me to have seats. We sat down and the officer sat at the head of the table. Officer Williams had a file with him; he opened it up and began to lay out papers. The officer spoke mostly to mom but also at me, he described the charges the state had filed against Walker, something regarding child pornography, abusing a position of power and using electronic devices for harmful personal gain and something about a minor, all the phrases were overwhelming and sounded frightening.

The officer said that it would take a lawyer to explain the risks of everything involved but these were the charges and what my attacker was facing. The officer said that a prosecuting attorney was on her way and that she would also need to speak with me, he offered to leave the room if I wasn't comfortable speaking with her in front of him. I began to get dizzy thinking about everything and was turning from nervous to shaky and scared, I tried to bury my eyes into the palms of my hands.

We continued to speak about what to expect in the upcoming few days, tomorrow held the first trial and that we had an appointment at zero nine hundred hours as an informal meet and greet with the rest of the legal team beforehand. The phone in the corner rang and the officer excused himself. He was a sturdy built man but seemed to flow silently as he walked in his shiny shoes around the room. Mom asked if I was ok and how I was holding up, she could tell I was nervous, she said I looked pale. Mom encouraged me to just breathe.

Officer Williams came back in with a mid-thirties lady, her light brown hair had highlights in it and it was tied back, she was in a pants suit with a pink striped shirt on underneath. She introduced herself as Lacy Brown and that she worked with the prosecuting attorney that would be going after Walker. She asked me to repeat the night in February, starting with the accident then on to the ambulance. She scribbled feverishly on a large yellow note pad and kept asking me details. I spoke about mom finding the blood smudge on my underwear and what I remembered as I spoke with Ms. Rollins.

I told her about the dreams and how some of them opened up more details like the camera clicking and seeing the phone over and over. I felt the lump in my throat grow as I told her about when the officer pulled out the same cellphone from the ambulance ride. Lacy pulled out the cellphone from a bag marked "evidence" and asked me to confirm that that was the phone I was talking about. Seeing that cellphone made my anxiety spike even more, I felt ill and I didn't like it.

Lacy kept asking me questions and also to repeat things I had said over and over again, it was annoying to have to repeat myself but I understood that she was being thorough. Lacy scribbled and jotted through three pages worth of notes and the four of us sat in the room for over an hour. She asked about Ms. Rollins and asked a lot of the same questions Rollins' had asked also. I felt uneasy talking about a lot of this but she told me that it was normal, as well as the same reason she was here there of some, sending a girl helped, even if only a little.

Lacy seemed sincere in her inquisition and I was glad she was on my side, or at least on the good side. She told me that Walker had hired a lawyer and was looking to try to bond out of jail for the time being. The judge denied his request because of the nature of the crimes but also because of the evidence against him. She warned me that a nice lady judge took a quick look at the pictures to determine the nature of them as well as the severity. The judge was unhappy that people like this existed. Lacy said that this was her third case like this this year already but not to the degree that a medical professional was involved.

I started feeling sick, I was so scared to be trapped in that car all wrecked and mangled, glass screaming all around me and when I finally had help, I became a victim all over again, in an even worse way. The anger inside of me beat against my chest, I could feel my temples swell at the thoughts of my undies and other things on his phone, the idea that he was sending the pictures of me to his friends made me want to scream. Tears welled up in my eyes and looking at mom, made her eyes well up also.

The conversation teetered off to its' end, Lacy shook our hands and left mom and I both a business card. She reminded us both that early the next morning we were all due in court. Officer Williams escorted us out; he also shook our hands and also ensured us that he would be there bright and early to walk into the court with us. I felt stronger knowing I had such a large badass in my corner and the fact that this football player sized man with a stern voice was also a cop made me a little more at safe. I hobbled out to the car, mom helped me get in and she was already peppering me with questions as we drove away.

Mom asked if I was hungry, well I was in fact, subway sounded fantastic at this moment in time. Mom wanted to know what my thoughts were about everything, how I felt about the morning to come and how my legs were feeling. I felt stronger every day on my legs, my arm pits were getting sore with these crutches rubbing them raw but I was doing well overall, at least physically, mentally I was still a mess.

I told mom about how nervous I was, scared but strong enough to want to show up to see this come to an end. I was still worried about the media and news people you see gathered all around and stuff like on TV, I was scared that I would be this public person that was molested and have my story told all over and that people would get the wrong idea that I was raped or had truly horrible things happen to me when it was pretty mild on the spectrum of things.

We made it home after a brief lunch and then I laid back down on the couch. I texted with Sara and told her about my meeting and asked her what her thoughts were on everything. Sara apologized a few times that this stuff happened to me and expressed how hard she wished it hadn't. I told her not to worry about this and that I was strong enough to get through it and that she needed to heal faster to be here with me. She laughed a bit and said she was healing as fast as she could, I smiled at her response.

I continued to talk to Sara and told her how I felt. I was worried and scared and freaking out over all of it, my head was spinning and I was tired. I let the background noise from the TV put me to sleep for a bit. Mom toiled in the kitchen and the light banging of pots and pans woke me as she prepared dinner. Mom asked me how I was doing and if I needed anything. I was doing as well as I could; given the circumstances. I wasn't feeling hot per say but I was going to stand tall anyways.

Dad came home and things almost felt semi half normal in a way, yes that was a roundabout feeling but it felt nice. We all missed Sara being with us but in a week or two she should be sitting on this couch instead of me and I'll be back in one piece and in school. We sat and ate dinner and each bite seemed a struggle to go down as there was still a looming lump in my throat. I was partially hoping dad would have grilled but moms' cooking was still top notch. I loved the mashed potatoes with gravy and baked chicken.

After dinner I helped mom wash the dishes, I had no problem standing to wash, the back and forth to clear the table was a less than easy task so I let dad be the man of the house and manage that task. Mom and Dad had a great relationship and partnership running a household and nothing was stereotypical; the man does this and mom does that type of stuff. Dad always did what he could to lessen moms work and mom sometimes let him while other times she raced to beat him to the tasks to give him a break.

I resumed my position on the couch and my butt imprint was right where I left it, it was settled in in all the right places, cradling and comfy. Moms' tastes in things were rather eclectic, the couches were dark green while the room had red trim and the room was also accented in dark reds, it was an off mix but it seemed to fit as if right out of a magazine. Mom was classy and tasteful in her life and we fit into it just right.

Mom rested on the floor and dad gave her one of his foot rubs, he rubbed her back with his big feet and whenever she seemed to drift off he'd sneak a toe under her nose only to get it slapped again and then they would both laugh a little. Mom looked funny laying on the floor and dad slapping her back with his feet while he laid back and flipped channels. Dad found some documentary on some ancient something or another and I was just glad to be back at home. I stared at mom and dad being goofy and they seemed glad to have half of their children back with them.

I smiled being home. I was grateful that I was no longer in the hospital but there were things like the monitor beeping that I seemed to miss. The background noises in the hallway had now become cars driving by and neighborhood dogs barking. The ambient noises that were and that now are, are totally different but more comforting. I was home and yet, I still felt out of place. I wasn't a stranger in my own home I was more like a stranger in a strange place, I became accustomed to the hospital in those five weeks but I also grew on my own accord. I didn't know I was changing when I was, I didn't know it until I got home.

The sky grew dark as the afternoon dwindled away. I didn't feel tired but I knew that I needed to try to sleep. It took me a few minutes to convince myself to get up, my body was warm and comfortable settled into my own impression on the couch. I ached as I got up but I made it with minimal effort. Mom asked me if I was turning in and if I needed any help, I told her I was ok and would manage, and I didn't want to interrupt her back rub, she and dad needed the time.

I hobbled up the stairs and grabbed pajamas then headed to the shower. Before I undressed, I stared at myself in the mirror, I no longer saw myself as the little girl I felt like, something in me changed again. I noticed I stood up straighter, especially after working the crutches all day. I tried to stand tall like Detective Williams, proud and ready to whoop ass if necessary.

I disrobed and had to undue the six Velcro straps keeping my leg brace squeezed onto my leg. I worked off my hoodie and looked at myself again; my collar bones stuck out and I could use about five more pounds on my frame. It's funny to think that I could use weight when so many girls out there struggle that they are to fat, well too skinny means easily pushed around.

I'm glad that I am petite while there is such a major problem with obesity. Being heavy would suck too, having to carry around an extra sixty or seventy pounds would just be tiring each day in and day out. I love being able to run and even though it burned my lungs and legs, my legs craved the unheeded ability right now. I stood there in my tank and undies and started my shower. I set my towel on the toilet lid for after the shower.

I looked at myself again in the mirror. My hips bones still jut out and I thought about those five pounds. I liked my body before, and now I loved it. My body took one hell of a beating and looking at it now I looked at it more machine like, not the bundle of biology all working together in a symbiotic relationship making me strong. I almost felt like one of those super army chicks that didn't take crap from anyone. My legs looked rough with the small scars where I had metal spikes holding the inner bones together and the knee scar from where they had to re-wire my quadriceps femoris muscle ligament back to it.

I flexed my knee bringing my heel to my butt and the knee felt funny but I think mostly sore form underuse. I eased into the shower and started my routine of washing my hair. I washed it slowly as with the rest of me, I was careful to not shift to much weight on my sore leg and kept a hand ready to grab the side of the tub in case my leg decided I needed to sit down without the rest of me being ready for it.

I leaned my forehead against the wall and let the shower just beat against my back, the water seemed to fall slowly and my hair slowly fell down my face too. I spat the water out that accumulated in the corners of my mouth and it still tasted a little soapy. The water was warm and the steam filled my lungs, I remembered the chemical burning in my lungs when I was trapped in the car accident, I tried to let the water wash away some of the awful memories and I knew that in time, the memories wouldn't go away, but cloud over with strength.

I kept my eyes closed and thought back to that night. I remembered hearing Sara and Katie choking on their own blood, the smells, the sounds, the flashes of headlights still crossed the insides of my eyeballs. I felt my body tense as the glass screams screeched in my ears, always following the bright flash of lights. I took a few deep breathes and tried to calm myself down. I felt the water fall down my legs and splash at my feet.

I changed my thoughts and tried to imagine what the morning held for me. I told myself that I would stand tall and even in the face of Walker and his animosity I would stare back. I can no longer be hurt; I am strong and have proven to myself that I can weather anything. I shook a bit at the thoughts of what was to come and I was nervous but I wasn't going to back down. The image in the mirror five minutes ago wasn't a little girl; I was no longer the eight year old I tried to hold onto.

I was in high school in another year; I used to think you became a woman physically there but mentally in college or even after. I felt myself more a women in my mind that I thought I might appear physically but even with the changes I noticed over the last few months, slowly developing and one day having hips, I knew I was closer to being a woman now than the little girl I was.

Tomorrow morning I will stand up in court, a woman, and do the right thing. I trusted myself to truly know what the right thing to do was and I assumed I'd know it when it was time. I took another steam filled breath, held it in, and then exhaled. The air was getting thick but I wasn't ready to be done with my shower yet. The beating water felt so relaxing on my skin. I felt my muscles slowly relax and I could feel my heart beat slow a bit, making my eyelids feel heavy.

The water began to run cold and I lifted my head to wash my face really quick before I froze. I stepped out of the shower carefully and toweled off. Mom knocked to check on me, startling a bit before I replied that I was ok. I stood in the mirror and brushed my hair, I stared at myself, looking for a difference in my eyes and face. My cheekbones stuck out a bit and my eyes sunk in a bit making me look tired. I didn't see anything difference in my eyes, I always noticed people's eyes and felt you could tell who they were by how they looked back at you.

I wondered what Walkers eyes looked like, would they be cold and look right through me or maybe he would hide his eyes in shame. I finished brushing my hair and slipped into my pajamas. I didn't strap my brace back on for the short strut back to my bed. I tossed my towel onto the shower rail to dry and pulled the door open. Mom was right around the corner and headed my way. I stood up straight and waited for her to embrace me.

Mom hugged me tightly and I hugged back. I was tired and sore from the day but her warm hug felt reassuring, that I was still her little girl. I wanted to cry one last time but told myself that I didn't need to right now; I was tired of crying for any reason except joy. I haven't cried for that in too long and if I was going to cry again anytime soon, that would be my reason why. I clenched my jaw and kissed mom on her cheek, she patted my back a bit.

Mom walked me to my bed with her arm around my back, supportive but not undermining my own strength and abilities. Dad shouted "goodnight Pea" from down stairs, we yelled for fun so I replied in kind. Mom laughed a bit and rung her ear with a finger then she yawned a bit while she was at it. I tucked in and mom sat on my bed as I settled in. Mom spoke to me and told me to get a good night sleep, she would be waking me up early to get dressed and fed as well as get us to the courthouse in the morning. Mom told me that dad was taking the day off and would be joining us also.

I quickly texted Sara goodnight and she wished me "good luck kiddo". I listened to a car drive by, it wasn't a cart traveling down a hallway but it did break the silence. Mom sat with me for a few more minutes, running her fingers through my hair and still talking about how I need to be strong and not show any emotion while in court. She wanted me to take an idea and hold it tightly, not to let anything rock me or my focus and that no matter what, to" be firm".

I sat in bed and ran through scenarios of things that may happen in the morning. I was curious about what was going to happen but I was also dreading the events to come. I was afraid to face my predator, I hated thinking of him like that, I would rather consider him a bully, a jerk, or some mean kid that does more than pull hair or spit on girls. I wonder if he was bored or had some fetish for younger girls, maybe he was just a guy and wasn't using his brain, I had so many questions, a small part of my curiosity almost wanted to talk to him and ask him some questions to help me sleep a little better.

I laid in bed, feeling the cold of the sheets turned warm, the bed supporting me; my wet hair warming and slowly drying. I strained to hear mom or dad talking but it was all quiet. My eyes slowly closed but it took longer for my mind to fade away.

chapter 19

I SHOT AWAKE Tuesday morning, that frightened awake like I slept through my alarm, the kind of waking that craps on the rest of your day. I knew today was going to be a whole different kind of day. I sat up and tried to rub my face to gather my bearings, I shook my head trying to hurry awake and have myself together. My stomach was already heavy as I remembered what was in store for me within the next few hours.

Mom was already up and moving around the house, I could hear her and dad talking downstairs. I grabbed my nice clothes and headed to the bathroom to wash my face and get ready. I stared myself down as I dressed. I wore my nice dress pants, a nice lacy tank under a suit coat, I put my hair into a low pony tail and added a bit of color to my face to hide the tired with minimal foundation. I strapped on my leg brace, I was worried it would wrinkle my pant leg but it was too bulky to fit underneath.

I carried my crutches down the stairs with me and used the rail to help ease me down one step at a time. Once at the bottom of the stairs I looked at the metal sticks in my hand, I carried them with me into the kitchen to join mom and dad. I sat at the table and made my good morning greetings. Dad was already in a suit as mom was also in a pants suit. I didn't have much of an appetite and already wanted to vomit. Mom poured me some raisin bran and I picked at it, I leave all the raisins for the end, save the best for last right?

Mom announced that it was time to get moving and the lump in my stomach started to twist. We loaded into the car and headed to court. I was nervous and felt all the blood drain from my face. I began to get dizzy and felt ever more ill. The drive wasn't nearly long enough;" I'm not ready to be here", I told mom and dad as we pulled in.

There was a lot of commotion on the front steps. There were small groups of people standing around, two camera crews for the local channel 4 and 7 news and the dread was overwhelming. I squeezed my leg muscles, a trick they taught us in track to avoid passing out; the muscles push blood back into your brain to help replace the loss. I climbed out of the car and braced myself for what was to come. I still wasn't graceful clambering out of the car; I just tried my best not to fall on my face.

Mom and dad took up position on each side of me as we walked in. I tried to put my mind at ease by picturing myself as Dorothy and we were traveling down the yellow brick road. That idea quickly left my mind as I heard the news reporters talking. I tried to avoid eye contact and prayed hard that I could make it into the building without being bothered. I wished I was invisible. I tried to avert my attention and hung my head down. I wished I had big sunglasses on, those stupid big ones that made girls look like bugs, to hide behind.

Mom reached for the door and let me in; Dad took her place holding the door as we made it into the court. "Lorna" I heard my voice called, I looked around and tried to see through the gobs of people to find its origin. Mom gave my arm a slight tug and to my left to where Lacy was sitting with another lady on a bench. I hobbled in their direction with mom and dad.

Lacy introduced us to a taller lady, she had shorter blonde hair and she introduced herself as Janine, the prosecuting attorney. My stomach seemed heavier as things progressed. Lacy, Janine, mom and dad spoke and asked questions back and forth. All of their jargon made me dizzy and confused. The crutches under my armpits rubbed against them and they were already raw and sweating.

Janine headed to the courtroom and left the four of us to muddle in the hallway for a few more minutes. Lacy told us that Janine was heading in to meet with the judge and the defense attorney before the trial hearing gets going. Mom kept me in the corner of her eyes and dad stood tall with his shoulders back. Dad cleared his throat signaling mom to walk back towards the door to greet Detective Williams as he entered.

Williams joined our group and asked how we each were doing this morning. I hung my head, looking at the floor searching for an appropriate response; I was at a loss so I just nodded. The officer and dad both stood tall and steady, mom seemed strong and confident but I felt meek and small standing with them. Lacy told us it was time. Now the dry throat turned to a lump that felt like a brick and it took me a second to get my momentum to follow the adults. Each crutched step felt like I was in quick sand, I felt like I wasn't moving any closer to the room as I tried to keep up.

The courtroom was monstrous with rows and rows of wood benches with marble columns lining the walls. There was a lady judge sitting in the bench at the front of the room watching everyone. She had short black hair and a pearl earring in each ear, she appeared to be mid -forties and had a pleasant smile on her face. I was asked to sit with mom and dad on the left side of the room in the benches towards the front. Each crutched step towards the front seemed to get harder and harder. Detective Williams sat in the bench right behind us and Lacy sat next to me, mom on my left and dad beside her. Janine took a seat at the table in front of us.

The judge stepped out through a door behind her chair and a second officer came out through another door towards the front of the room. There was an officer on each side of the judge's bench now, each dressed in brown sheriffs' uniforms, hands crossed over one another at their waist. My heart beat pulsed in my chest as well as my throat. The heart beats made my temples pulse, I could hear the "lub dub" of my heart louder than the other noises in the room, it almost echoed in my ears.

Suddenly the door towards the front of the room opened and another officer came through, following him was a short stocky man with short buzzed hair, the younger guy shuffled through. He was in an orange jumpsuit, his hands were handcuffed to his waist and his legs were also handcuffed. I assumed that that was him; that was Walker. Everyone's head turned and watch him make his way to the other table over on the right of the courtroom. My pulse grew stronger; I felt my anger and fear race each other through my head.

I tried to turn away but I wanted to see his eyes. I wanted him to look at me and I wanted to know what kind of look it would have been. He sat down for a moment and just hung his head. He seemed rather clean cut and athletic in build. There were a few people sitting behind him, I guessed they were his parents, maybe friends. I immediately started trying to see if one of them might look at me, maybe one of them had seen my private pictures and might look me up to associate those pictures with the young lady sitting here. I tried to peek out of the corner of my eye without staring or getting caught staring. I was scared.

The bailiff guys stood taller and one began to speak loudly to address the whole room. "Please rise" he said, mom helped me to stand and the rest of the whole courtroom audience stood up also. Being a judge has to be hard but it was pretty cool that everyone has to stand when told and the respect that the judge gets is pretty awesome. The judge came back out of her door and told us all to be seated, everyone sat back down.

The bailiff spoke loudly to the judge, "State of Michigan verses Walker B. Chaudry" I got a bit dizzy listening to all of this stuff and it blurred a bit. Walker stood up and spoke his full name: "Walker Brian Chaudry" she asked him if he understood the charges against him, he nodded and replied "yes Ma'am" then sat back down. Janine stood up and told the judge that that the charges were in line with the actions spoken about and the evidence presented before court.

Janine spoke more legal stuff and it was too much to try to keep up with. Walker sat there with his head hanging low, breathing shallowly. The judge asked Walker if he had anything to say before she began. He looked up, nodded, and then stood up. Walker tried to stand up tall but his head kept drifting to the floor. He cleared his throat really hard before he began to speak. His voice wasn't anything special, just sounded like any normal guy but it had a crackle in it. I guess the man I created in my mind was much more of a monster that the one I stared at.

The bench full of people that sat behind Walker all hung their heads as he began to speak. Walker took a deep breath, "You're honor" he preceded his statement with. "I made a dumb choice, I am young and I am guilty" he stated. The judge asked him if that was all, he told her he had one more thing to say, he said "I'm really sorry" as he turned and looked to me, he apologized, His eyes were sad and tears streamed from both of them.

My head spun as the rest of the session sped along. Everything seemed to blur until the judge whacked her gavel on the bench, demanding my attention. People began to talk; there was a bunch of noise and commotion that seemed almost deafening. I tried asking mom what all was happening but I couldn't even hear myself, let alone her. There were people moving and standing, there was an older lady crying on the other side. I felt bad for her that she was crying, I never meant for any of this to happen.

Mom hugged me tightly and kept telling me that everything was ok. I didn't know what was happening. I was lost, confused, rampant with emotions and wasn't sure why. In the hour we sat in the courthouse a lot seemed to happen, yet nothing happened. A lot of people sat in this room, silently, with little movement, gazing at the judge the whole time. I didn't notice many people moving except maybe to adjust an article of clothing or to tug down a riding shirt.

I only recognized a few people in this room, I wondered who all everyone was, what their purpose was, what they were all here for. I wasn't a confrontational girl, I wanted to be strong and sit here like a statue, but I felt like warm goo on the inside, my stomach hurt and my head pounded. Lacy gave me a shoulder bump in a motion to let me know that things were about done. She leaned to me and told me that this was a preliminary hearing but that he admitted guilt but it also meant that I may not need to come back at all.

I like that I wouldn't have to come back and I could get to forgetting all of this mess. There were so many people and it was overwhelming. The commotion continued as mom helped me to my feet. Everyone stood as the judge stood and exited through her door again. A sheriff made his way to Walker and escorted him out of the room. I looked at mom and told her I wanted to talk to him.

The words squeaked out of me but her eyes told me that she understood me. She leaned forward and asked Janine if it was at all possible. Janine hurried to the suited man that stayed at the table that Walker sat at. Janine nodded as the man got up and hurried out the door. Lacy asked me why I wanted to talk to him. Lacy told me that this was unheard of and unnecessary but also confirmed that I was certain.

Mom asked me what I was doing and if I was sure also. I nodded and swallowed to choke back the tears. I just had to know why. I told mom that I wanted her with me, Lacy and Janine wouldn't let me alone either. The suited man was waiting for us outside the back room door that we had come in through. The man nodded his head to a side hallway for us to head towards.

I and my entourage of well-dressed people all followed him. We walked down the hallway and the judge came out a door on the left side, the suited man told her about my request and asked her if she approved the request. The judge looked at me, her stare made me feel tiny. My anxiety rushed through me and I tried to shake my nerves and told her I wanted to ask him one question. I stood up tall and stopped leaning on my crutches when I answered her.

The judge looked at me for another minute, I took a deep breath and I told her "just one question" with assertiveness. I took a deep breath again and followed the judge and the sheriff a little further down the hall. There was a door, a big wood door, the last one on the right. The door was marked "inmate holding". The sheriff unlocked the door and let us in. Janine let the other lawyer guy enter first, she followed and the judge led in mom and I, Dad stood just inside the door.

Walker sat in a small cage located in the corner of the room with his head hung low, his elbows on his knees and his head on his hands. The man addressed him and asked him to stand. I hid behind Janine when the judge spoke to him. "You don't have to answer anything and you can refuse all of this if you'd like, I'm only hear to get a better angle on everything." Walker stood up and nodded, tears still streaming down his face.

The lawyers parted from in front of me and I stood there looking at him. He wasn't much taller than me, maybe early twenties, his eyes red from crying, his light brown hair buzzed pretty short. The orange jumpsuit hung on him, like the chains did. My head felt heavy but I cleared my throat. "Why" I asked him, "how could you", his whole demeanor just sunk, like the air was let out of him.

Without raising his head he just said "I'm so sorry". I repeated my question "why" again but with more rage. Walker continued to stare at the ground; he told us that he had earlier been at a hospital dropping of another patient. He had stepped out to a railing to smoke a cigarette and there was a surgeon smoking some pot. The doctor said that now that "the medical cards were out that it was no big deal". He joined the doctor in the joint as the surgeon was calming his nerves before the upcoming surgery.

Walker continued talking, he said that he hadn't really smoked much before but that sometimes the nights get rough and some of the accidents can fray to your nerves. The joint calmed him but also left him pretty buzzed. He said that after he got back in the ambulance they got the call about our accident. I felt my hands shaking but I wanted him to keep talking as I tightened my hold on the hand grips of the crutches.

The judge told walker that he could stop talking anytime he wanted but that it was his choice. Walker just nodded and said "yes ma'am I know" he finished by telling us that he had no idea how old I was and that things were a little foggy from the drugs. He said he had no excuse for what he had done. He was burned out from long school days and long work nights. He apologized again. His head hung even lower as he sniffled to keep clearing his nose.

His lawyer handed him a tissue to blow his nose through the squares in the cage. Walker spoke up again; "Ma'am, I am responsible and will handle anything you decide that I deserve" he turned to me and lifted his head and spoke again, my head was spinning and my legs felt like jelly. "Miss, I truly am sorry, what I did was unforgivable, I would like you to just not let it get in your way, not to let this be a moment that alters your life as it has mine, I'm truly so deeply sorry, more than you'll ever know".

Walker hung his head again, mom started to weep a little. The sheriffs stood like those marble columns in the courtroom, the judge shifted her weight from one leg to the other as she listened. I cleared my throat and only muttered "It's forgiven" I wasn't sure I meant it at the time but knew that in time it would be. This, of all things that night was insignificant. I found much strength from that night, this small moment, an act that Walker had made in a drugged haze of stupidity, wasn't going to define me or my life.

If I were to ever be free from this mental prison, forgiveness would be the key, my ticket to a free life. I knew that being in prison would be Walkers' binds for a very long time but that guilt would be his chains forever. I couldn't let this be my chains also. I was going to be one of the few people in this world that could truly forgive; I refused to be a victim for the rest of my life. Being strong enough to forgive is an attribute of the strong and damn it all, I will be that strong, some day.

I stood there, half leaning on my crutches, I stared down Walker and just watched him sigh and breathe for another minute. I still had so much I wanted to know but knew deep down that there was no way of ever truly knowing everything. I turned around and headed for the door. The lawyer and judge both thanked Walker for taking the time. Dad held the door for everyone to exit. I heard one of the sheriffs tell Walker that transport would be here soon to pick him up.

I could hear the shackles on Walker jingle as he sat back down. I crutched back down the hallway. I heard the heavy footsteps of many of the dress shoes following me, there was no cadence with all of the steps but I tried to keep a good pace. The hallway seemed to go on forever. Looking around the corner I saw more people coming in through the metal detectors and all dressed in suits and nice clothes.

Janine came up beside me and thanked me for coming. She and Lacy both shook my hand and bid me a good day then walked back down the other hallway talking between themselves. A sheriff walked past us and back into the courtroom. Mom and dad each took up position on either side of me quietly for a moment. Dad asked if we were ready to go. Mom let out a big sigh and agreed that it was time, time to go home.

We made our way out the door, past the metal detector and the group of sheriffs standing at the ready. A short sheriff with a salt and peppered mustache told us to have a good day then quickly turned back to his station at the metal detector. A news lady holding a microphone walked towards us, mom intercepted her quickly by just saying "we're here for a parking ticket" and the news lady bought it and turned back around. Mom wasn't usually a liar but she had a good reason and did so without her nervous lip bite or any other facial expression upon her return.

We gathered back into Moms silver fusion and that's when my eyes watered. I was so scared and yet I held up, I faced the man that assaulted me, took advantage of a barely conscious young girl, and I didn't back down.

It was weird, I could feel myself smiling and crying at the same time, it was like that contradictory Michigan conundrum of sunshine and rain. I had so many emotions running through me. I was so very relieved too; I was finally done with this crap, out of the hospital and done with court crap. I wanted to collapse.

I felt such a huge sense of relief; I leaned my head back against the headrest in the car and seemed to exhale for minutes. I fumbled for my phone to text Sara that it was all over. I shook as I tried to text and spell correctly. I smiled larger as I read, then reread my own text, "all done, it's over with" I just began to cry, this was the happy cry I had been waiting for, for a long time. Mom cried a little in the back, dad drove us all home.

Dad told me that he was proud of me and that it had to take guts to walk in that courtroom and I did it like a lady, tall and secure in myself. I felt my heart lift and the weight of my chest go away. I was truly free of that night. I felt like I had suddenly been miles away, thousands of them. Instantly the world felt ginormous again, this huge world that presents itself when you travel across it or return from its' other side or something.

chapter 20

I SPENT THE rest of that day rethinking about the morning. Things seemed to streak by the rest of that week also. I spent most of it with my butt on the couch. Mom returned to work Wednesday and left me by my lonesome now that I was getting around better. Sara got some news that she would be home the following Tuesday, one week after my court date.

Mr. Matt still came over one or two nights a week to hang with dad in the garage, he occasionally joined us for dinner now and then as the weeks turned to months following our ordeal. Sara made it home and also spent a week recovering and Ryann stayed with her that week helping her around. I returned to school and spent a week crutching around. Bobbi said she saw me briefly on the background of the one news report about the trial.

Things calmed down and slowly returned to normal at home and at school. My school seemed both large and small, much as the world did during the court date. I seemed to have lived a whole other life between the accident and the court date. I felt like a whole new person, or at least a newer modified version of whom I once was, I hardly recognized who I used to be.

In the end Walker was sentence to five to ten years for the sexual misconduct on a minor using a digital device. The judge granted him some lenience because he was completely cooperative and also on drugs at the time. It scares me to think that because pot is now becoming legal that surgeons are hopped up on it and operating on people. It's sad to think that so many people think that drugs are plenty ok and also that they become a crutch for life when things get tough.

I finished out my school year; it was uncomfortable at first returning to school. I heard few whispers here and there during the next few weeks, kids mentioning "it's her" and mixes of "that's the girl". The first few times my head turned to see who was saying what, held my head up higher and just remembered that I stared down a man nine years older than me and that none of these poser kids could bother me.

It took a while but the sudden glass screams got farther and farther apart as I slept. Sara and I started running again in the summer. I missed being in track with Bobbi but I sat bleacher side during the meets and cheered on my best friend. As the summer came and went I had the notion to visit Walker once and check in on him, out of curiosity but instead I called Lacy for an update.

Lacy said that he was still safely locked up but finished his degree online for biology. I was glad that he didn't turn out the scumbag monster I originally pictured him to be. I sometimes wondered why I wondered about him but put it out of my mind just as quickly as those lights veered at us in that car. Mom and Dad went back to their lives and we seldom spoke about everything that happened.

I sat outback on the lounge chair a lot, the buzzing of the bug zapper was soothing and I still watched the trees sway. I always felt better with a light breeze, Katie making the trees dance like she had at the concert. That night still plays in my mind a lot, I always force myself to think about the concert more than everything that happened after we left the parking lot.

I found a newspaper article of the accident, as well as one about Walkers' sentencing and saved them, for me. My scars slowly healed but never went away. Sara got stronger and we both ran during the summer. Sara loved running, I wasn't that big of a fan a year ago but running now felt freeing, strengthening. I never again felt like the little girl I was at the beginning of the year, like a piñata after Cinco de Mayo, beaten.

Every night before my shower I stare at myself in the mirror. I look at myself looking back. You never know how you will age and suddenly one day you wake up and notice you are a woman. I left childhood behind me abruptly in February. I sent thank you cards to everyone I could remember at the hospital that guided me back to health, that shared a part of themselves with me to find myself.

Naiya went on to write me back and let me know she was accepted into med school and was glad to hear I was doing very well. She was encouraged to become a pediatric doctor and I sometimes wondered if her story about that little boy gave her the strength it did to me. I jotted in this journal originally to make the glass screams go away, I now reread it every so often to relive what I went through. Every word I read put me back in the hospital, getting stronger.

I was admitted a frightened little girl but over those few weeks the cocoon broke and I found out I was so much stronger than I had ever imagined. No longer a feeble girl in my mind, I was a strong girl and that could never be taken away from me.

Sara spent more time hanging out with Kelly and we occasionally spoke of Katie. The three of us vowed to keep Katie's memory alive, and that we would all name our first born daughters after her. Ryann decided to stop mulling around and enrolled at a community college and decided to pursue culinary arts. As high school began, it was if things had never happened but Sara and I would never forget.